About the Author

Tameh Kuczynski has been writing since she was thirteen, it was a middle school play which she wrote/directed and also played a character. The 'Writer' life chose her, she has been writing ever since. Also, she is a poet and canvas artist, traveling and discovering runs deep as well. Life unspools itself and she writes about what she sees and feels, and a writer who prefers fiction that is so believable the reader will be entranced with characters. She is Polish and those roots run deep.

The Boy from The East

Tameh Kuczynski

The Boy from The East

Olympia Publishers
London

www.olympiapublishers.com
OLYMPIA PAPERBACK EDITION

Copyright © Tameh Kuczynski 2023

The right of Tameh Kuczynski to be identified as author of
this work has been asserted in accordance with sections 77 and 78
of the Copyright, Designs and Patents Act 1988.

All Rights Reserved

No reproduction, copy or transmission of this publication
may be made without written permission.
No paragraph of this publication may be reproduced,
copied or transmitted save with the written permission of the
publisher, or in accordance with the provisions
of the Copyright Act 1956 (as amended).

Any person who commits any unauthorized act in relation to
this publication may be liable to criminal
prosecution and civil claims for damage.

A CIP catalogue record for this title is
available from the British Library.

ISBN: 978-1-80439-061-0

This is a work of fiction.
Names, characters, places and incidents originate from the writer's
imagination. Any resemblance to actual persons, living or dead, is
purely coincidental.

First Published in 2023

Olympia Publishers
Tallis House
2 Tallis Street
London
EC4Y 0AB

Printed in Great Britain

Dedication

I dedicate this book to family and to my father, who showed me the path of hope and making dreams true.

Introduction

This tender story takes place in the last bit of the final years of World War II. It concerns Hober, a young boy born into the hardships of the Polish tundra, the premature death of his entire family due to accidental fire during the annual harvest festival in his home village of Hoslava, life in the depth of wartime, and the unity of village life from one invasion and season to the next.

Time transforms into seasons; life is gauged by planting and harvesting. The harvest festival begins in an innocent manner and ends in the ash and rubble of burned out homes, the tragedy taking place long before war can make its way to the village. Winter is locked in heavy winds, blowing the embers about as if they are confetti, taking away years of simple prosperity, along with lives. The only survivor in the family, Hober, is lucky enough to run away from the flames – yet unlucky enough to lose everything dear to him.

Hober's shock leaves him dazed and stranded as nightfall comes quickly; even for a child such as he, there is little shelter for the village people. He rubs his dark brown hair while drying the tears from his round blue eyes. When daylight arrives, they will start to rebuild, bury the dead, and survive as they always have, united. Hober is truly lost, though, suddenly exposed to life without his parents' guiding hand. He falls asleep under the free-forming stars, sheltered under a wintergreen pine, occasionally snuggling against a welcoming farm animal.

As the night skies fill with vivid shades of blue, Hober searches for the conviction to survive. Inside the heavy weighted doors of the Orthodox church, he learns better survival skills from the village, himself once an orphan who understood the loneliness into which the world can wrap one.

Hober survives without perceiving the passage of time in hours and minutes, the modern sense. He instead gauges time by the sun and its risings and settings. Day turns quickly to night in winter, while summer days are long and often, in a sense, much harder. Winter holds the settlers in wanted captivity to their eaves and hearths for a time of family unity and reconnection after the hard-working days of summer.

Hard work is a common thing in the village, truly the order of the day: sowing seeds, darning clothing, churning milk to butter, drinking root tea to burn away winter's storage of fatty foods that aid in the insulation of the body. It is also a time for creating pottery of Polish blues, earthenware gifted from the soil. Though young, Hober is already part of that hard-working tradition. His arms might not be large beneath his woolen sweaters, but they are already trim and muscular.

The hearths that devour the wood logs quickly need perpetual restocking during summer days that begin with first light. "Lucy" is the term for light, the name of a precious saint that protects the small village. The round, full sun brings with it the arising of village life, embedding soil under each palm, the villagers their great unity for the earth like cloth.

Hober has grown a bit frightened by village life since the fire. He chooses to live on the edge of the village as a partial recluse. He needs to become more with the natural world, to heal, to figure out what happened. Nature begins to become his surrogate family, even though it had a hand in killing his blood family with wind gusts and red-hot embers.

There is a fine line between nature and man.
    Summer gives him an easier life. Under the umbrella blue sky, it is easier to find shelter. Autumn is not as kind; at the tail end, she brings winter storms that challenge Hober and his makeshift forest living among the great wolf, bear, and ominous forest walls. His deep connection with the life-giving earth keeps him in much needed focus.

Chapter One

Under the broad sky, amid the chaos of the fire, Hober stares at the skeletal structure that was once his home. All that remains appears as ribs and protruding bones coming straight from the earth, his entire family now gone. He recalls his sister's sense of humor, his mother's gentle ways, and his father's large working hands dedicated to family. Still in great shock, Hober sits with his face to his palm, smudging ash on his cheek. He runs a hand through his coffee-colored hair. He sits in a half-burned chair, facing the west window overlooking the tundra, where he used to play the violin to his mother. She lent it to him after she inherited it during better times. Hober's love for the outdoors kept him from becoming a master violinist, yet inside, the boy who is soon to be a man decides he *will* survive. His love of nature delivers life lessons only out of mutual love, and he uses that knowledge to better himself.

Several years back, the Bishop of Warsaw came to visit the village, leaving behind profound words: "Empty hands in idle times leave one with an empty heart. Family and kinships are nurtured with the earth as we are truly one, one in all to survive this life." Hober has never forgotten those words. His mother used to claim, "Hober, I swear if I had your way, you would be in the tundra daily, building stick bridges to the other side of the brook or hanging from the strongest branch upside down, only to view life in a new way." Hober just gave her a grin when she said such things. He could not deny what she said... what she said was the truth.

Every mother wished for her children to leave the village and live in Warsaw, the city of opportunity... as it once was, before the war. They wanted their children to perform in opera houses or grand cafes. These children had very little time for dreams of their futures; that was up to their mothers. Fields and farms consume their time, yet dreams always survive.

After the fire dims, Hober finds himself very tired, physically and mentally. All is lost, eaten up by the flames. All the family belongings are lost to the fire as well. He has nothing but a knapsack and bed roll he found after the fire was worn out by its own backdraft. Most villagers bunk down inside the church, on the floors or in the pews, but Hober wants to be alone. He camps on the edge of the village. The stars light the sky over the tundra, a sad low glow casting shadows into the trees as a lone wolf howls from the dense forest. The sound, somehow, gives Hober a sense of companionship.

Hober wipes away the smudges of embers from his face, never to shed another tear. There is no time for crying, words his grandmother said to him on occasion. He keeps these words near him; if he shows any weakness, it could be the end.

The next morning at first light, the villagers begin to clear the burned rubble and piles upon piles of stone, making way for new homes and fields of better crops. For most, their houses are spared, the wood lace trim around their front doors reminding them of how quaint and tightly knit the village is, in good times and bad. They are used to regularly rebuilding and restructuring their lives from invaders, politicians and others who have attempted to claim their land at one time or another. The villagers are filled with pride and determination for their homeland, which they also honor by painting red birds and other symbols of nature on their houses. A small brook flanks the village, while vast fields sweep toward the foothills and towering peaks of the Carpathian Mountains.

Like most in Hoslava, Hober's family was not well off. They never left the village for exotic places like Russia and Moscow. Instead, they struggled to do their best at educating their children and raising them in the love of God and faith and hard work. Now winter grows close and the villagers prepare as the mountains are already covered in snow.

Soon, Hober is lost from public sight. Everyone seems to be fending for themselves, though disaster can create bad behavior in some. The first rule of village life is to take care of each other. The approaching winter adds more fight-or-flight to the people's minds, a dimension of chaos they are used to. Yet hope keeps them living on the tundra.

The church opens its doors to those in need, its bell chiming faithfully on the hour beneath the welcoming Orthodox cross. Like Hoslava itself, the church is small and cozy, painted white with a slanted roof. Hober stuffs his pride in his wool pocket and asks the priest if he can lend a hand with food and shelter. Father Dominik, once an orphan himself, recalls the hardships of being alone. He rubs his cleanly shaved chin, extends his robed arm and gladly helps Hober, preparing him a place on the floor and some bread with milk. Hober looks up at the church altar, which proudly showcases the Slavic crucifix that hangs broadly to the small church altar, the gold dome keeping it safe – or as safe as war and the seasons will allow. This gives Hober a sense of belonging again, a sense of home, the crucifix the symbol of hope.

Only a few days until winter arrives. Hober sits by his favorite hardwood tree, choosing the strongest branch that leans over the village center. He makes it his vantage point to eavesdrop on local gossip. He forms his next move, speculating and thinking things through... where to find better shelter? He needs to build better shelter as autumn exits and winter forces itself into the village.

His heart fills with deep, aching sorrow. He misses his family, his sisters teasing him and his mother's voice of reason, his father's eyes and patience. Hober longs for his father's teachings on how to be a better man. He sees his father's hands in his own, equally strong, and wonders if he will live up to his image. A few women walk beneath Hober, unsuspecting of the child spider in the tree, speaking of the ceremony for those lost to the fire. His heart bursts open with pain and love, the loss of love that will last a lifetime.

The sky seems void of clouds, blank like some faces who lost everything. The embers flung themselves to "life" as the wooden rooftops caught fire quickly, the backdraft sweeping the walls, collapsing them inward atop families. This fire had a wicked way!

Hober flicks the hair out of his eyes and climbs from the tree and walks to the church. A flier is pasted to the doors, giving notice of the ceremony and a meal following. He can't bear to face the reality of such loss. He turns his back and walks to the forest edge, where he listens to the sounds of the birds and small animals rustling through the undergrowth for food. He feels a kinship. He too feels animal-like as he searches for food in the village, not keen on killing anything that also survives as he does. The dampness in the forest feels inviting, the diffuse light bringing out blue tones in the pines, the color of winter. He listens to the brook as it speaks to him in tongues of renewal and youth. This is his place now.

In Hoslava, the people gather what they can for the ceremony and meal: cabbages, a few eggs, some potatoes, sausage, and warm braided bread. Soon, evening skirts the horizon, and the ceremony begins. Hober's stomach growls and rumbles, reminding him of his hunger. He drops his pride and enters the church, where a few women are holding pine wreaths as Father Dominik calls out the people who were overcome by the fire. The women are covered respectfully as the scent of incense blankets the church. Hober feels God's presence, which eases some of his pain. The people place their hands over their hearts in memory of those lost. Afterwards, the hearty ceremonial meal gives nourishment and lifts their weight of loss yet knowing war will soon be at their doors. Turbulence is a way of life.

The church bell chimes the noontime hour as Hober leaves the ceremony and makes a bed inside the sheep stable. He lays there, counting the slivers of moonlight coming in through the cracks of the shed. One beam seems to balance on his chest. He places his hand in front of the beam, playing hide and seek. This draws him back to family, his sisters' laughter and obvious protection of the only boy in the family other than their father. He starts feeling lost again to loss.

Later, in a dream, he sees himself walking from the village to the mountains, where he finds glaciers that never turn to liquid, the tundra lit by large overhead lights, and barbed wire placed at borders once free and open. He screams himself awake in a cold sweat! The moon beam twinkles off the medal his father gave him, an old medal hanging from a copper chain handed down by his grandfather. He again feels the presence of those gone before him. "You are brave, Hober!" ancestors whisper in his ear.

He falls back asleep, dreaming of Angelica, her long golden blonde hair wrapped in braids, the natural blush of her cheeks. His sense of loneliness becomes more apparent, even in dreams…

Dawn breaks with a few snowflakes drifting casually to the ground. Hober's eyes adjust to the white snow and brightness of it all. He sees the foothills completely covered, the Tatras lost to a winter haze.

Winter and war seem to be hand-in-hand, though the village has not been touched by war in a half century. They have been blessed and lucky enough to not be in its belly, but realize luck can run out, just like time will. Every so often, a disheveled soldier reminds them, walking through the village, lost. Or, a horse with no rider gallops through the village center as the empty train departing to the cities, only to bring back with it… *war.*

Parts of Europe fall to the frost and frozen rain as Siberia blows her breath to the south, halting all movements of travel. The village is hunkered down as Hober continues to search for permanent shelter. As villagers smoke fish from the glacier lake, the scent drifts through the village and Hober's hunger pangs once more hold him captive. He now knows he can only rely on himself, too proud to ask for more help from Father Dominik.

Hober pulls his wool coat closer to his face. A few

buttons pop into the snow. He tucks his hands in his pockets and feels the crucifix lying there safely. He rubs it between his fingers and thumb, praying out loud, praying for shelter and the ending of war and the beginning of love! Afterward, he finds a bale of hay and tucks himself deep into the heart of it, falling quickly asleep. Winter then makes fun of him, bouncing an empty tin to his feet, startling the boy. The snow is now three feet deep, surrounding him in nothing but cold, the loneliness overwhelming.

Daylight brings the winds that whistle in ghostly song as they whirl around the shed, waking Hober. After he gathers his belongings, he steps outside the shed door to find a piece of Polish blue and white material. Inside is one egg, the symbol for luck – and nourishment – and a piece of cheese. He scratches his chin in doubt, wondering who was so kind to make this gesture! "Who would have known I was here? The shed has been empty since the fire!" he asks out loud.

Soon, it doesn't matter. Once he tastes the cheese and bread, and the whites of the eggs… it was God sent.

After finishing his simple meal, Hober gazes to the last sign of autumn, the stubborn leaves still clinging hopelessly to the thin branches at the top of the tree. They begin to spin and flip, the sign of a fierce storm approaching, something his sweet grandfather taught him before he died of wonderful old age.

The slanted roofs are now plastered down with snow. The chimneys puff away as the smoke drifts upwards and out into the open sky. Hober admires nature's ability in just *being*. Nature has a way to make humans feel reclusive, withdrawn from the division of nature and man.

Chapter Two

Lars is Hober's best friend, the only friend he truly trusts. They sit for hours discussing the world beyond the mountains, and life beyond war. Hober snugs his collar closer to his neck, his ears nearly frozen from the brutal North winds. He feels his head for the Polish blue and white wooly hat his grandmother knitted him, but he touches only hair. The hat was lost to the fire and irreplaceable.

Hober's grandmother passed away five years ago. He could truly use a hug and a knitted hat from her now. He cuffs his hands to his ears, muttering under his breath; his breath is seen in the frosted day. "Grandmother, I could use a new hat and all the hugs you have to give!" he yells.

While lost in his vocal prayer, someone asks, "Are you cold, Hober?" A deep thinker and a bit sarcastic at times, he thinks to himself, *Who would ask such a silly question? Any time a person sees their own breath, that means it is COLD!*

Lars begins to laugh nervously, his impish green eyes open in surprise. Angelica has found the two nearly frozen. She flirts with Hober in her own way, her long locks bouncing, her blue eyes alive and dancing, spunky and lively as ever. She's sending him all the signals of flirting – yet Hober is too young to recognize these signals. He squints his eyes, adjusting to all of the white of the snow and sky. Once in focus, he visualizes Angelica standing there with arms folded.

"Hober and Lars, are you both idiots?" she asks. "Do you want to be frostbitten? The mountains are as if frozen bosoms and there is no time for silliness!"

Angelica is several years older than them. A student of literature and poetry, she tries to use her poetic prose on the boys.

Lars is the youngest of five children, the baby of the family. Hober is a bit more mature and taller, but neither is tall for his age. Lars claims constantly that if another war was to break out, he would enlist and fight the enemy, making war sound as if it were a heroic thing to wish for. He has no idea of the ugliness of wartime. Lars' father and Hober's had worked together at the mill and gotten to know each other, a friendship the boys feel they should carry on. Their fathers worked deep in a forest so dark and dense it never saw true daylight, a closed canopy pines and hardwoods shading the forest floor. Many were lost in what the men named the "Forest of the Unseen". It struck fear in most, except for Hober.

Lars and Hober make a pact and promise to remain friends for life, no matter where the winds of events and history take them.

Being defiant and mischievous, Lars takes some cinnamon candles from his mother's candy bowl, tucking them into his pocket for Hober. He welcomes the sweet warm sensation of the cinnamon and hugs Lars for his generosity. Siena, Lars' sister, begins to call him back home for a midday meal, leaving Hober to roll the candy inside his mouth as he stands alone again. "Hober, my friend, I will see you later or tomorrow, come find me when you can!" Lars yells as he waves goodbye and runs off into his warm home.

Angelica crosses the snowy village center to the church, past the houses sitting close together, all with slanted roofs and small front doors. Hober watches her intently. A strange feeling comes over him, one he had never felt for anyone... *what is it? Is this what love feels like?* Hober follows her into the church, where the veil of incense drapes around the pillars of marble and statues of saints. He cautiously whispers to her, "What is it you pray for?"

The question surprises her. "Well, I pray for those now and those of the past, funny Hober!" she replies with a twinge of sarcasm. He should know what she prays for, she implies. He knows her well enough by now!

Hober's face turns a few shades of red, embarrassed. His eyes open widely, eyes that fill with the sad compassion of his heart, and also the things he needs to know and do to stay alive. He could have thought of a better opening line. He stands closer to her, the heavy wooden doors of the church creaking and popping under the weight of the snow. The doors sway in and out as the wind blows out the candles. Night seems to fall more quickly... or perhaps another storm was approaching.

His heart racing, Hober leans into Angelica and kisses her, not knowing the romantic "dos" and "don'ts". Angelica throws her hair over her shoulder as her eyes suddenly turn into blue ice. She leaves the church abruptly, apparently upset, not saying a word... yet halfway home, her eyes melt and she breaks into a smile. She understands why he kissed her, and why he did it in the church. What better or more sacred place to show true feelings, to show love in the only way he knew how?

As Angelica walks away, Hober thinks how much her full lips tasted like Lenten bread, sweet and delicate. He smiles, happy he took the risk of giving her a kiss! No need to be ashamed. God was watching, so it was okay and not forbidden. It felt good to love again.

Father Dominik smiles, too; he watched from behind the stained glass like an unseen chaperone. This makes him smile, for Hober has love again in his life and heart. Angelica's footprints are inside the doorway of the church. The doors permanently left a gap after expanding during the summer months, allowing the snow to cover the floor lightly like a blanket, holding her footprints. Father Dominik smiles even more as he closes the doors tightly. He too feels something special for Angelica, a more mature, manly depth to it than young Hober yet knows. However, he will never let his feelings be known. Orthodoxy allows and encourages priests to marry and have children. If he is to be with someone, Father Dominik realizes, it will have to be the woman who becomes his wife.

Life is lonely on the tundra when living alone. Hoslava prepares for nightfall. Villagers stay inside as winter stirs and lifts the wooden shingles, allowing drafts to enter. The squirrels, rabbits, fox, deer and other creatures of the forest and tundra also find shelter as a hard gust howls from the mountain and down the foothills into the village. Shortly thereafter, an avalanche thunders downward, a reminder that no one survives without showing plenty of respect and skill.

Wool blankets and heavy curtains hold out the better part of the cold. Mothers keep their *babushkas* on while they rest, in respect to their position as the matriarchs of their families. Father Dominik, though, is a kind man; he allows the intermingling of men and women during mass. There is no segregation in the village, either; they all work together. The shock of the fire slowly becomes a past memory.

The lights begin to flicker. Winter and war have pulled the one powerline down; it sags to the earth. The candlelit scent of wax and flame ignites the darkness. Communication with the outside world could very well be potluck now, or perhaps a lonely soldier making his way to the village, receiving a blessing from Father Dominik as the drifting soldier tells of the horrors of war and the great, great loss! The backbone to village life keeps them going, praying and caring for each other, along with drifters now and then.

Father Dominik never turns a blind eye to anyone. The orphanage taught him that life lesson after his family was cleared away like eggs by the German army, each member sent off to the camps. His heart only carries mercy for those who do such horrible things. The bloodletting of war and death showed that nothing is permanent. Rebuilding the village and spirits while praying for the departed is their only life, simple and clean and clear. War is ugly!

Night falls, weighty and heavy from a day of snow and ice. The night sky is shaded in winter blue, the color of progress and hope. The whitest star illuminates the shadows of the forest, seeming to crawl on the ground as it ran from the mountains and avalanches.

With another day ended, there is still no permanence to Hober's lodgings. He lays on a pew, hand chiseled from Rutka, a small village specializing in wood craftsmanship. He falls into a temporary, coma type of sleep, with jerking movements, restless as images from the fire flash before him like a film from a cinema.

Hober awakens to winds and loneliness once more. This time, he feels as if his spirit is beginning to sink, though picturing Angelica's face and dreaming of a future keeps him hopeful of threading a life together.

Lars skirts off to his warm home, siblings bursting with chatter, the long family table set with a green ribboned cloth and earthenware holding the clearest spring water. His family sits discussing life, which gives Lars a door to bring up Hober and his dilemma.

"Mother, Father, Hober is alone and cold and very hungry," he says. "Can we bring him into the home for a short period of time, please?" Lars knows this is asking too much, with food minimal for the large family during winter.

"Lars, my sweet boy, we too care for Hober, and I would bring him in if it weren't for the rations we now have to live on. The war is taking away supplies of food after we run out of what we have stored. We need to look after ourselves first."

This leaves Lars with an odd feeling. The war he so desperately wants to be a part of is now revealing its ugliest side. His youth is so clear in the way he weighs life and the importance of it all!

Hober awakens to the voice of Father Dominik. "Would you like some food?" he asks. The church fills with the scents of butter-colored candles and warm wax. Father Dominik waves his hand above the food, blessing it first before Hober takes it to his lips. A few sugar cookies twinkle. Hober devours them quickly, as the sugar clings to his lips. He then thinks of his last confession, and the kindness Father Dominik shows him… *it is time for a new confession, maybe a trade-off for the food.* But Hober knows he lives strongly in faith.

"Father, I suppose it's time for me to tell you my trespasses," Hober quietly says as the father nods in agreement. "Father, forgive me for I have sinned. I truly can't recall my last confession, but I am willing to begin with now. First, I took a fishing line from Lars when we were fishing at Black Silk Lake. I caught the largest fish that day and felt guilty for this, so I gave the fish to Lars for his family. Secondly, I told a white lie to my mother about some dumplings I took from the pantry for a trek into the forest. When she asked if I took them, I said, 'No, maybe Father did!' I tried to blame my father, and now, he is no more!

"Thirdly, I kissed Angelica here in church, and I truly liked it and the way she felt, her lips are sweet and soft, and I… well… I just liked it and would do it again."

Father Dominik smiled at Hober and told him his penance: to fish again using his own line, and to give what he catches to Lars' family. Hober isn't keen on killing anything, though; this time, he will let the fish lie on the shoreline until they breathe no more.

"Also," Father Dominik continues, "pray for your lies you said to your parents and never ever kiss Angelica in church again." Truth be told, he feels a little jealous of Hober's kiss with Angelica, he too sensing a need for confession.

After the confession, Hober leaves the church, thanking Father Dominik for all his kindnesses. The pews creak in the shifting of the church, Hober crosses himself in the Orthodox way, forehead to sternum, then right to left, counting the mosaics on the floor as he leaves. The icons appear to listen to Hober counting out the tiles, the gold spires holding the candles with layers of wax, each representing ages of the past. As he does so, Hober holds the wooden crucifix his father gave him, the Black Forest wood crucifix on the copper chain.

Suddenly, the air feels laced in anguish as he thinks once again of his family. *Thank God for Lars and Father Dominik. And Angelica. If it weren't for them, I would truly be alone in a world that seems to pay little mind to the lonely ones.*

The snow begins to form tall, solid drifts that appear to be barriers outlining the village in the dim light of winter. Long-distance storms from Siberia and the crashing sounds of avalanches mingle with the church bell as it chimes. The season of clarity has arrived, winter as crystal clear as fish swimming upstream on a warm summer day.

The village lays exposed to the challenges of the snow. The howling of the winds and a wolf drown out the distant crashing of ice from the mountains. Hober, again, sleeps inside the church, and in the pews, finds a pair of wool gloves left behind by a churchgoer. He places his fingers and palms into the warm spun wool, happily clasping his hands to his face, warming his cheeks. He can hear the snow layering itself onto the church roof tiles. The wooden eaves crack again. There is always that sound to a church, as if someone is there with you, even when the church is empty.

Saint Lucy gazes at Hober behind her dark hair and pale eyes. The icons wink to him for a job well done thus far. Hober thinks of his friends, safe and warm in their homes. He rubs his jacket button through his fingers. His mother made the buttons and coat; her love still protects him, now and forever. He knows it will soon be time to leave the church and make his own way, creating a shelter, perhaps one inside the forest. He will welcome all the animals to his doorstep, from the great bear and his wisdom to the sparrows that willingly nest in the dark canopy of the tallest trees. They, too, search for a better vantage point as Hober climbs the tallest trees in better weather to get another view of this world.

Outside of it, war explodes, the bombs and noise so devastating most men and women learn to live like mice beneath the buildings, keeping to the cellars and passageways under the cities. He realizes his life isn't nearly as bad as those who deal with war directly in their faces and souls.

By midday, all vision is obscured, blurred and shaded by snow and more snow. Ice sheets make it look like a fairy tale. The trees are sugared with ice string candy, in the imaginations of the children. They snap under the pressure of the heavy, suffocating ice, and the church takes on the image of a Christmas card blanketed gently in snow. There is no movement in the village.

Hober makes his way to Lars' woodshed. The forest didn't invite him to stay the night, as the winds ache inside Hober's ears; he can barely feel his nose. He opens the woodshed door and sits by a pile of wood, hoping and praying somehow Lars will know he is there and will ask him inside, near the hearth of drying clothes and family discussion. The winds crackle in a voice of their own, mocking Hober: *Poor little one half frozen, poor Hober!* He feels and hears the loud, cruel winds. He tucks his pant legs into his boots and cuffs his collar around his neck, then walks directly to Lars' front door.

Angelica watches from her window. She created a small porthole from the frost on it to watch Hober walk in the sea of snow.

Suddenly, everything is quiet. The snowstorm settles down as Hober knocks on Lars' door. The whole family knows from the tone of the knock that it is Hober, still searching for shelter.

Lars opens the door, pulling in Hober and slamming the door quickly behind him.

"Jesus, Hober, what are you doing?" he asks sharply.

Lars' mother gasps at his usage of the Lord's name in vain. "Lars, you speak like that one more time, you and the lard soap will become best friends, as I will wash your mouth with it!" she says.

"Oh, he has heard before mother!"

"I'm not kidding, Lars," she replies.

Hober is half frozen. He begins to cry, his first real tears since the fire. He holds his hand in his palm as though he has a cruel toothache, when really, it is his heart that aches.

"I don't know what to do or where to go," he says aloud while sobbing. "I feel lost every day, no matter where I am, this is killing me as well. I miss my family and have no idea what to do with the love I have for them. I feel as if I could die, too!" The sad, tearful sound of his voice speaks more than his words.

Lars' mother holds him close. She insists that he remove his jacket, and leads him to a chair at the table. "Eat, Hober, eat," she says. "I am sorry we haven't invited you sooner. You understand the brutality of our winters, and food is to be rationed. Please, I want you to eat whatever you need. Our home is yours for the night."

Hober wipes his tears away. They rest on his wool sleeve. He eats and eats, feeling a little better, accepting the hugs from Lars' mother. Hober truly needed this gift, the unity and substance provided by the food, the companionship of Polish lie.

After dinner, Lars and Hober play several rounds of chess. As the clock strikes eleven, they decide to call it a night. Outside, the avalanches sound closer than usual. *The mountains just can't get up and walk closer to the village*, Hober thought, yet something odd was taking place, odd sounds and sensations as the ground shimmied in recurring explosions. They lit up the night sky into bright orange in the distance. The tundra was again under the firefly glow of something very large… war? Fire? Both? *Ice cannot form fire; how is this possible?* All these thoughts ran through Hober's mind like a ticker tape at the German stock market.

Soon enough, they had their answer: the next village caught fire due to the explosion of ammunition secretly stored in the dry shed. The village and surrounding forest burst into flames; even in the heavy snowstorm, the flames took and took! Hober begins to shake. The reminder of what was taken from him and his fellow villagers comes too soon.

Knowing Hober would be in distress, Angelica packs a small cloth sack with eggs and bread as well as a small bowl of borscht, steaming ruby beets and small pieces of meat. The best way to cure sorrow, she knows, is through food and love. This is her poetic heart speaking to her, her way of showing Hober gentle love.

She wraps herself into a checkered blanket, pulling it over her head as she makes her way to Lars' home. When she arrives, she knocks frantically to get out of the cold. Lars opens the door, pulling her in as he'd done to Hober. "Are you crazy coming out in the storm?" he asks. "Do you not see the village next to us is on fire? What is so dire that you need to be here now?"

Lars is partially yelling, which pulls Hober into the room. "Angelica! What in the name of God… why are you here?" He mimics Lars' tone.

"Well, Hober, I am here to check on *you*, silly boy!" She is angry. Lars' mother gives her a look at suggests, *Dear God, even my own boy can be daft in silly questions!*

Angelica is clearly concerned for Hober. The flames from the next village illuminate everything in an odd hue of orange. The sky looks as if it fell into the night and is melting the snow from the village. Thinking of that, Hober is impressed at Angelica's stoutness. He walks to her, giving her a hug so strong it could have come from the forest bear!

The three spend the rest of the night discussing next future steps as the nearby village continues burning to the ground, eventually leaving no traces other than smudges of tar-like images on the white snow. They open up the sweets Angelica has brought, easing Hober's doubt that all things are safe now. She also brings out some milk and rice with brown sugar, a few dumplings and cream, and slices of an autumn apple she kept in the box under the fire. Fresh fruit is a luxury in the winter! They enjoy the gifts, licking their fingers, grateful for her way of being a nurturer. Hober likes her even more now.

Like the snow itself, night drifts into the next day. A heavy smoke cloud hangs over the village that smells of plastic and toxins, not wood from the forest. The fire that took the nearby village also burned their last bits of petrol and supplies stored for winter. The survivors walk by, knowing it will do no good to ask for help, since Hober's village is still recovering from the autumn fire. They head back into the snow and disappear. Lars trembles at the thought that perhaps soldiers will cross ways with these poor souls, taking them into the heart of war and the barbed wire strung throughout the tundra, creating makeshift borders to keep village people in and the world out.

What a fine line, life. Death can come at any moment from anything larger than the villagers, yet the mountains are not as cruel as some men in soldiers' uniforms.

The winds curl around the trees, shaking loose the last leaves outside Lars' home. The air is crisp, the scents of plastic and petrol gone, a freshness hinting at spring, the first signs of blossoming life to come once the north wind quits blowing. Up in the mountains, winter will last several more months. The glacial lakes high above never thaw.

Hober feels relief. The worst is behind them and it's time to paint a new life canvas. He, Angelica, Lars and Father Dominik will make a difference in the village, in one way or another. It is never spoken about in the outside world. There is not much written history except that of past invaders from rich countries, and the countless wars that once made the people nomadic, living a gypsy life until they resettled on the tundra, built Hoslava, and accepted its natural challenges, trials and tribulations.

What they found was what kept Hober hopeful: village life is the unity of spirit with the flesh of the earth.

Chapter Three

The Tatra Mountains overlook a broad valley filled with sunflowers, daisies, lilies of the valley and milkweed, dictating life to those living in the tundra beneath the foothills as time passes on. Hober, now a young man, is finely tuned to the natural world and the village people. Angelica longs to be a nursemaid and to leave the one-powerline Hoslava for the big city and education at university. Her books of poetry and literature line her bedroom walls, her desire for learning stronger than Hober's and Lars'. However, all three are totally dedicated to faith, their friendship, and the villagers.

The war is nearly over. Scars will remain as time births new days, then shuts tired eyes when those days change to nightfall. The rumbling of avalanches never ceases, as the shifting ice is heard loudly, no matter where the villagers go. The sound embeds deeply into their souls.

Father Dominik rings the Sunday bells. He also rings the bells in reminder of the life and times dedicated to the village people, the seasons that give bounty, the lakes that supply fresh water and fish… all things to be very thankful for. The church doors are always open to those in need as the mountains shelter the forest and the edges of other countries in their shadows. There is no easy passage over the mountains, nor to the next country. Hober regularly thinks about it.

The seasons always leave a trace of their own powers, no matter what. Summer is warm and often dry, leaving the villagers to carry water for distances to the village. Autumn brings the chance of fire, quick angry fires, while winter carries lofting snow and sideways storms. The mountains command nothing but respect; very few make it through the foothills, let alone the Tatra mountain range.

"God is good!" This was always the villagers' war cry as they fought off war and invaders, only to rebuild and grow. Father Dominik falls even more deeply in love with Angelica, a love he must always keep within his heart, never telling a soul of his love and desire nor his want for children and the simple life of the tundra. To some, this is a small world, but to others, it is as large as the world truly needs to be.

The war is ending. It will be a long time until the wounds close and mend. Men roam aimlessly, while prisoners of war held captive by their own men walk into the village, telling of the death and the stench, the crimes of war, the beauty of their passage to the village, the healing soil of the tundra and the caring people who hand out warm drinks and slices of bread. No one wants to see anyone suffer any longer. Hearts are heavy, yet hearts repair. In human need, we can all pull ourselves a little closer to each other.

Hober writes this message onto a piece of paper he keeps folded and tucked inside his coat pocket, profound words from a survivor, his heart mending with each day that passes, each prospect for a better future held in the dawn. Hober often writes about the winter and forest, the pale blue lake seemingly sheer as the fish swim, gulping plankton, the trees bending to the winds of the North.

Life changes, but slowly and gently. It subsides in its need to be clear about the primary ruler of the tundra. Hober sits in a tree in the afternoons listening to the elders speak, the pine wreath that signifies life and death, those gone before and yet to be born.

Around him, birds are busy finding good and nesting, the finches and crows calling forth loudly, mourning doves cooing beautifully while sparrows flit through the air. High overhead, a falcon soars in circles, searching the ground for field mice or small rabbits.

Inside, time is spent kneading dough and flouring tables for rolling out dumplings, the barrels filled with fresh cucumbers and vinegar-scented cloth in the kitchens. Hober often thinks he could never leave such a place to play violin in a posh café while facing the busy city streets of the West. This is home, the soil underneath his nails, his heart soaring free like the hawk, his eyesight keen on everything that surrounds him, the watchful mountains. Life is life, and it is a good life.

Angelica sits on the bench at the rail station. One train comes at least every two weeks as the faces of city people flash by in their suits of herringbone. The women wear hats that look like icing on a cake. She envies life away from the village, university halls lined with books. She no longer feels that love and marriage are her first priorities; studies now consume her desire. The desire to become better. Village life may soon be behind her.

Hober notices Angelica's distance and lack of affection. He is still in love with her, but she never wants to share time with him and Lars. He knows she is drifting away to the city life and he cannot stand in her way, since nature proves you can never imprison the free. Lars still talks about enlisting, even though peace needs to heal those that war took from. He is eager to be a part of something much larger, it pesters him in a childlike way.

The three talk amongst each other, but this time, it is more of a mature discussion. This talk is about Father Dominik and his life of being alone without no spouse. Angelica suggests the day should be shared over warm milk and dumplings, since food is the binding agent for friends and family. They walk to the church, spreading open the doors, peering inside the half-lit building as Father Dominik stands from prayer.

"What a motley crew!" he says. "What I can do for my young friends today?"

"Well then, Father, can you ask the dear Lord to place me where I am more needed?" Hober laughs at Lars' wisecrack comment. "The village now can stand on its own two feet and I am simply bored!"

Used to Lars' mouthiness, Father Dominik shrugs his shoulders. "Hober, now do you think I can work miracles? Or is it the miracles of God you seek?"

This stumps Lars and leaves him speechless and quiet. Hober giggles at Father's comment; after all, he is only human himself!

They walk outside, blessing themselves before stepping down the church stairs. The air is fresh, the sun beaming happily. Hober always feels the connection with earth and air, forest and animals, a gift not many are blessed with. They wander toward the last melting pile of snow, and stir away a small flock of crows plucking at it for seed. They place their hands over the blue coolness while looking upward to the mountains. Father Dominik spots the daylight star, the planet Venus, and asks her to guide those lost to the war to their earthly, or heavenly, home. "The mountains appear so very small today," Angelica says. "The sky is swallowing them inside the midst!"

Hober declares that the mountains are always in control. So is the forest, the same forest that has swallowed men whole and houses the great bear who swallows all the bad children of Hoslava! Father Dominik laughs aloud, a good belly laugh, as Lars squishes up his face. "Oh, my grandmother used to say that to me so I would behave!" They all begin good belly laughs. Village folklore never leaves you, no matter your age.

The war seems far away, but the cold reality of its evilness is clear. The economy shrivels to a survival level, and many revert to the old style of living – living off the land and by the hands on your body. Petrol is scarce, so many farmers use oxen and carts, with big black rubber wheels made of replacing the heartier wooden spoke wheels. Life rolls on, despite its surprising punches!

The *kishka* binds families at the dinner table, which Father Dominik longs for as he tells his three friends about the loneliness he carries. Once in love with Angelica, he now needs to find a wife and have children with whom to share the *kishka*.

Lars pulls from his pocket two round pucks of blood pudding. Nothing in the village goes to waste. "Anyone want some?" he asks.

"Gross, Lars! How long have they been in your pocket?" Hober asks.

"Not long enough, in my book."

They all begin to laugh once more. A loud crash interrupts their laughter. The mountains shift and move once again.

The trees give life as well, the sap being used for glue and food, the fields now plush with fuzzy growth popping up from under the ground. Change takes place nearly every moment of the day. Love, too, changes with the young and their lifetime desires.

Father Dominik asks all of them to pray for each other, never stopping, always keeping in touch. It feels like a premonition to Hober. What is it Father truly wants to say? It leaves Hober feeling a bit odd… is Father going somewhere? If so, where and why? He has always been inquisitive; his own father told him regularly, "Hober has a need to know."

Father Dominik has a plan for his future. He may head south one day and say goodbye to the village. Finding a wife is more difficult than he imagined, and time seems to be running short on starting a family. The war has killed more than anyone realizes. Men in the masses are now gone, the male census in short supply. Many women are now widows and in need of men to help run farms and homes. Priests are scarce as well to the outside world. The Bishop of Warsaw keeps Father Dominik updated regularly on the war's devastation and great loss of life. The Germans killed many priests of all kinds – Catholics, Orthodox and Jewish rabbis – holy men that never did any harm. They were wiped out in a spray of bullets. This leads Father Dominik to think he can do a better job in the cities, perhaps marrying and having children to raise in the mystical beliefs of Orthodoxy that family and earth are truly one under God.

Hober will lose a great friend in Father. They have become very close in their orphan kinship, as well as the long walks they take in early evenings when the seasons will allow. Their discussions focus on the meaning of life and each person who lives on the planet, on nature and the ties that bind them to the soil, along with discussions on other countries far and near. Hober is infatuated with the United States for the power and kindness they showed in the war, along with Great Britain. He feels a unity and strength of will to show some form of gratitude. Perhaps one day he will have the chance to give something back to the people who left an impression on him.

Angelica fixes a midday meal. Her parents' kitchen is small yet wonderful, and the dining table handmade by her grandfather of sturdy walnut. The colors of the table give great warmth to the house. The curtains are made of heavy linen striped red and white, almost as if it were leftover material from handstitched napkins. The fireplace sits in the center of the house and can be seen from the sitting room to the kitchen. Tins perch on a thin shelf, while the off-white dinner plates are stacked on a flat board shelf.

Angelica is eager to show off her cooking skills to Lars, Hober and Father Dominik; likewise, they are eager to be the official testers of her cooking. The house fills with aromas of flour and sweet butter as the stove is stoked with wood every fifteen minutes while preparing foods to be placed inside the belly of the great red-knobbed stove. Her visitors sit at the table, their hands folded together, anticipation beginning to get the better of them. Or is it their stomachs?

The old clock that sits on the mantle clacks away: it is one in the afternoon. The kettle bubbles over for their root tea as everyone stands while Angelica finds her way to the table. The food rests in earthenware bowls and platters waiting to be plucked. The three young men fill their stomachs with equally full smiles, making Angelica very, very happy. One day, she decides, she will make a good wife after beginning her career in the city. Children? Perhaps one day, but it is not one of her priorities. She keeps that secret to herself.

Afterwards, Father Dominik heads back to church to give a short mass dedicated to the soldiers of war. Everyone has suffered, and there is truly no winner at war! He rings the church bells to start the mass, which is attended by villagers not working the fields. "This mass, brothers and sisters, is for all the soldiers of war," he begins. "It is for the German men who were ambushed into becoming soldiers, the Russians who also were ambushed into becoming soldiers, and all the men who are soldiers. We pray for you in the age of ages."

"Amen," the villagers say, but frown and whisper from the mention of the Germans. The enemy!

"These men are not all monsters," Father Dominik continues. "The mothers of these men weep for the loss of their boys! We cannot slight them in their anguish. War is ugly; war takes away irreplaceable souls. War has two sides and takes so many in such number, the dead lying in makeshift graves, the families who will never know the plight of some, the gravestones marked 'The Unknown Soldier' dotting all the fields and farmlands of Europe and beyond. The loss is great, one that should never be forgotten."

As he listens, Hober feels the breeze of spring, the scent of daffodils and the blooming of all things into green. The glaciers shine brightly, reflecting the early sun as it meanders into longer and longer days.

The mass ends with Father Dominik giving everyone a blessing for the upcoming crops season. The air is still crisp and clean scent of snow lingers in the tundra. All villagers are repairing their farm tools and roofs, a bit of tidying to the village center. There is a hum amongst the people. Spring is awake and she brings all her possibilities, the long winter now past, the time of divine unity sending a pulse through the people. They know life may become a little harder, but they also know idle time dissolves the hearty soul.

The few horses still at the village grow sick and die. The war has already taken their livestock; there are no replacements. The villagers cherish each animal and the gifts the earth gives to them. The unity of the earth and man is a clear thing. Every day, they realize they stand on the line between living and not surviving.

Spring dances in on the lake waters, rippling the sun as the fish swim freely, released by the melting ice. The favorite time of year for Hober and Lars. They spend as much time as possible fishing at the black silk lake. Hober catches and releases every fish; he relates to the gulping fish trying to survive. He can only imagine the horror his family went through when their oxygen turned to fire and they suffocated...

Lars threads his line first, dropping it into the clear water. The fish swim in schools, the lake well-stocked; not many villagers have time for fishing. Lars, however, is great at sneaking off, trying his best not to do as much work as he should. Hober drops his line, and the boys sit back to an old log that is now green from the damp terrain. Bright green moss covers the log as they sit happily and comfortably.

Lars catches the first fish, tucking it into a wicker basket. It tries to jump out for survival, upsetting Hober. Lars ignores the lid flopping open and the wide open mouth of the fish facing him, as if to say, "Help! What did we ever do to you?" Hober looks away.

"Hober, grow some backbone," Lars says teasingly. "Fish are for eating, and the best fish for eating are the ones that are smoked, with a bowl of dumplings and a few pears! Don't worry, they can't feel a thing."

Hober ignores Lars as well, keeping his concentration on the mountains and sky, enjoying the beauty of the beginning of spring. Glaciers are visible from the lake, the white that never fades, perpetual ice sheets that are the only constant thing he knows.

The afternoon trickles in. It reminds the boys they need to return to the village. Lars needs to help his father mend a few fences as the fish bounce up and down in the wicker basket. Hober knows he has nowhere he needs to be. It leaves him with a sadness.

As Lars and Hober walk the edge of the woods and field, they see a slumped man walking. It appears he is injured; he wears a gray uniform. The German is as young as they are, very empty-eyed. A sad sight, Hober thinks. It alarms Lars, who initially was excited at the sight of the soldier, since he had always wanted to be one. He runs to the soldier, now slumped halfway over. "Where are you going? Are you lost?" he asks in Polish.

The soldier seems to have an idea what Lars is asking. "I'm not sure where I am, or how I got to be here," he says.

"You are close to the Tatra Mountains, the border of the countries," Lars says, "but you are heading in the wrong direction... towards Germany."

"I have no interest in returning to Germany. It is tainted, all rubble, and I no longer trust the leaders of the country. I only want peace."

Hober sits on the ground, his head in his palm, the perpetual "thinking" stance. His signature look. "What is your name?" he asks. "Tell us about the war. Where were you last? Here in Poland you may come across freedom fighters who will shoot you straightaway!"

The soldier remains blank-faced. Nothing can trouble him now; he has seen the worst that men can do to each other. He interacts with Hober, his voice dull and lifeless, as if the drain to his heart was pulled like a plug and his innards poured out along the way. "I have been along the borders, fighting against the Americans. So much death, the air smelled of death, the ground was death, everything around me was death!"

Lars lets out a sound of disgust. He had no idea how bad war truly was.

Pity fills Hober as he looks to the soldier. "You can have our food and water if you want," he says. "Also, I have a knapsack you can take with you. It's warm and will tide you over until you end up where you decide to go." Hober wants so badly to ask the soldier in detail what exactly he saw, yet he knows it is disrespectful.

"My name is Fritz Kluger," the soldier said. "I am eighteen and now have nowhere to go. I belong nowhere!"

"You belong anywhere you want to be," Hober replies. "Stay here if you'd like. We can burn your uniform and tell the villagers you came from the next village over, which was just burned in an explosion. They will never know the truth...

right Lars?"

Lars is wide-eyed, his mind flitting with thoughts, the what-ifs. What if someone found out they were helping the enemy? However, was he? Once war ends, there are no longer enemies, are there? Some soldiers become wanderers and homeless, empty people trying to find a way to start over again.

Feeling great empathy, Hober gives the soldier his pack with his wool gloves and food. Fritz begins to cry. "Why? Why would you help me?" he asks.

"Are you not human? We all do things we shouldn't, and we all learn from the things we do, good or bad. Don't worry about the past any more. Pray for the future, and pray for the souls of those you killed. Start forgiving yourself."

Kluger breaks down, his tears turning to wails, a human opera of pure tragedy. "I killed under orders," he says. "I killed those who were doing nothing but trying to survive. I killed the innocent and the religious, priests and clergy, Jews and non-Jews. I killed so many they are all now faceless to me. How can I repent such things? Hell has no pity – and I belong in hell!" He is beyond distraught.

Lars felt the need to do something to break up the heaviness of the conversation. He ran and jumped into the icy lake, screaming like a girl. Hober and Fritz began to laugh, the soldier through his teary eyes, and Lars joined them – but was he cold!

The day dims as the forest begins to come alive, the animals beginning their evening sounds, the great wolf and her pack howling from the hills, the trusty woodpecker pecking away frantically at its home in the tree. Hober and Lars say goodbye to the soldier and watch him walk into the pitch-black forest. Fritz seems to have no fear of any predators waiting inside the woods. Perhaps he felt justice would be served if the bear took him to his den, and that would be the last of Fritz Kugler.

The dark sky is alight in a purple hue, the sun no longer visible. The boys remark on the beauty of the church's silhouette against Hoslava's few lights. The one power line is restored, yet many villagers continue to light oil lamps, not trusting how reliable modern ways are.

Slena, Lars' mother, is frantic. She has called him for a solid hour to return home, but he and Hober are out of calling distance. She hears nothing. Fishing is a time away from the drudgery of work, or so temporarily as Father Dominik repeats the Bishop's words: "Idle hands don't help anyone!"

The air begins to become crisp again. The night air of spring never truly warms until July. The scent of fires inside the wooden, close together homes of Hoslava blends with the chill, bringing Hober back to family again… the long table and his sisters' laughter, Father poking the embers of the fire as Mother separates the cheese from the milky fluids and places it on a plate of radishes and beets. He remembers the smell of cabbage boiling on the stove and the warmth of the house. Then his thoughts switch to the soldier they encountered, now also an orphan. He prays for Fritz and forgives within himself.

Hober reflects back to the woodpecker. He pokes Lars as they walk to the archway of Lars' home. "I would like to be a woodpecker, Lars. I would!"

"Why?" Lars chuckles. "And what animal *don't* you want to be? You are sometimes a bit odd, my friend, but you are my friend and I wish you to be a woodpecker pecking away at a hollow tree, eating bugs and flying free!"

Lars always feels the sense that Hober never truly wants to leave. His loneliness is obvious… why wouldn't it be? He has lost everyone – and is lost himself at times.

Hober nudges Lars, the gesture that he has gone way off-track. It sounds a bit like he was making fun of Hober, too. "Goodnight, Lars." He gives Lars a hug and walks away, kicking up a tuft of dirt. He looks back to Lars' home and the lights of the village, then finally makes a bed again inside the blacksmith shed.

Hober thinks about the day and all it gave – the German soldier Fritz, fishing in the lake, the mountains, the contrast between war and life… and freedom. He thinks of the faces of those placed in camps, the Soviets forcing uncles and brothers to become soldiers fighting against their own families. He thinks of the barbwire that remains, never to rust away and decay. The constant struggle of the Polish people to just *be,* the non-existing passageway through the mountains that unifies countries and expand populations, growth in faith and God. He thinks of the woodpecker and his endless need to peck-peck-peck, peck at anything that makes a hollow sound, unless he chooses a tree that sounds very solid. Is the woodpecker challenging himself? What creature doesn't face its own mortality and question its own survival?

By now, Hober already is showing the mind of a philosopher, a thinker, a problem solver… yet still a boy who misses the nurturing of his family. Love is not flighty. Love is what keeps us all grounded. Hober knows what he loves – the earth vibrations he can feel as he tills the fields, the knowledge he can survive the tundra. Respect for nature is a must.

He lies in the hay again as the church bells chime. Father Dominik gives the bells an extra ring, his six-foot frame providing added leverage, the added ring no doubt confusing the villagers. Hober knows the extra ring is for him. He falls asleep with a smile on his face, feeling loved.

A new day begins. Hober promised Padoik he would help clear a few trees from the southern quarter of his field. He shows up at Padoik's home as soon as the roosters give their morning call, so early the sun hasn't risen quite fully. Padoik is pleased to see Hober eager to get to work, already marking the trees with ribbons. The trees will be used as wood for building new homes, shingles and to stoke fireplaces in the winter. Some trees need to be removed as a blight is killing them. Hober marks those trees and listens to the slow creaking sound of the falling trees as the elder men bring them down. Hober's job is to further cut the logs into timber. The women remain inside, tending to a good spring cleaning, and the children and their education. In the distance, he can hear the plucking of violin strings, a young body learning the Old World ways. The violin is a poet musically telling a story of long ago.

The buzzing saws lead to a short day as the men work together, making a clearing for summer crops. Hober finds joy in the hard work as the mountains chatter with the last hair-raising avalanche of the season. "One day, I will witness first hand an avalanche and view the thundering power under the weight of the snow," Hober says to himself, "the letting loose of ice and sound."

The spring gets under Hober's skin, burying itself into his veins. As he grows, he feels a deeper connection with nature, a deeper longing to live among the animals and rolling tundra. A scholar he will never be; his mother always wanted him to be a scholar or a world-renowned violinist. That dream is long in the past.

Hober works a few odd jobs and purchases better camping equipment when he can find time to walk to the next village, where they sell used war surplus, small tents and tins, hiking gear and walking sticks. He also buys a few crampons and an ice axe, equipment for a mountaineer, even though he has never been to the foothills of the Tatra. There is also the odd Luger now and then, a skull etched into the wooden handle. A Nazi's gun. This angers him, especially since he was so forgiving to the young soldier Fritz. Stories of the war continue to trickle into the village, horrible, nightmarish stories that would be very hard to believe if not directly told by eyewitnesses. The villagers are peaceful, but when they hear of the betrayals and brutality that have befallen the people of Poland, their minds brew with anger.

Hober takes a map and studies the countries on the other side of the mountains, especially Hungary and Czechoslovakia, brother countries with which he feels a strong kinship.

Spring is religious feast time. Filling the village tables are foods like the basket S'wieconka, which contains Kielbasa, the life-giving egg, along with salt and pepper and bread. Bilberry leaves scent the homes, and life begins anew on the tundra. Ox carts pull wood to doorsteps, the carts decorated in light pinks and blues, along with ribbons of white. A celebration is at hand.

Lars' mother stirs the Kwasnica soup while looking back at Hober. "Please, Hober, stay for a meal," she says. He eagerly accepts her offer and places his pack in the small hallway of the sitting room. He walks to the kitchen, where the family is already gathered around the table. He pulls out a wicker-bottom chair and sits to something he has missed for years… a family meal.

Spring flowers decorate the center of the table, light blue and pale white flowers filing the earthenware vase. A few glasses shine from the window ledge as Hober scans the family home. Lars interrupts him by bringing up the fact that Father Dominik has decided to leave the village for Krakow.

Hober drops his cutlery. "What? What did you say, Lars? Father decided to leave? He never once mentioned that to me!"

"Well, Hober, did you think he would stay here in this tiny village that is going nowhere forever?" Lars asks.

"Yes, I did."

"He is handing over the parish to Father Miesko from Serbia," Lars says. Hober's heart sinks. Why did he still believe no one would ever leave such a small village?

After dinner, Lars' older brother, Artur, invites Hober to sit by the fire as they discuss their futures. Artur is leaving soon for London to become a solicitor. The law he studies will include the law of the Geneva Convention, which protect those who are captured as prisoners of war. Hober finds this interesting, and also sad. Everyone will soon be gone from the village, he reasons, making new futures for themselves.

Lars' mother carries in a tray of sweet cakes called Babka, and coffee for the men. The aroma fills the home with familiarity. Hober truly doesn't want to leave, wishing again family were just down the lane, waiting for him to return from Lars' home and tell a story of the forest. He doesn't want to grow older if it means others will leave.

Meanwhile, Angelica bakes Makowiec, a poppy seed roll. During the war, they squeezed poppy seeds as an opiate, to use as medicine. With no sterile hospitals on the battlefield, the seeds came in handy as a makeshift morphine when removing shattered limbs. Angelica wraps the Makowiec inside cheese cloth and walks it over to the church, a gift for Father Dominik, soon to depart for Britain. "Father, I will miss you terribly," she says.

She had no plans to say that. It just flew out of her mouth like a Spring butterfly flying from a buttercup.

Father Dominik thanks her for the wonderful gift, and then leans in to kiss her. Angelica backs away, not willing to allow herself to be involved. "Father, I wish you would have made some advance a year or so ago," she says. "Now you leave, and I won't move to Britain!"

The Father's face turns several shades of red. "Angelica, I will never forget you. I love you, and that love will be waiting for you in London if you ever change your mind." She can do nothing but to turn to leave. She does not look back to see his face one last time, nor does she have any self-doubt. Hober is the one she loves, and even he may not hold her to the tundra…

Angelica's young sister, Kutia, overhears the conversation. She has come to the church to pray, but now has a thing or two to say to Angelica but won't interfere. Each of them has to make their own way.

Now it's time for Father Dominik to say his toughest farewell, to Hober. Lars is a special friend, but not yet as close as Hober. He will be told afterward, or perhaps Hober will let him know that Father has left. Their walks to the forest, Lars' silly way of making them all laugh, Father's wisdom that never ceases yet never feels pushed upon them. Their memories will always bind them. Nowhere in the world will ever be too far for them to reach each other if needed. They accept each other for exactly who they are.

Travel is finally a bit easier, but the scars of war are still very obvious. The railway has cleared most of the unexploded bombs so shattered steam engines can make the path to Europe more accessible. Great Britain remained suspicious of Continental travelers who could be spies plotting some future invasion. After all, the Germans dropped bombs shaped like butterflies, the English children picked up the "toys", and were maimed or killed. The English are suspicious of Eastern Europe, with good reason.

Chapter Four

Life returns to normal after Father Dominik leaves. In other words, plenty of hard work. Hober is more deeply drawn to the forest, while Lars is preoccupied with a village girl who just moved from Russia. Her beauty captivates the young men. Angelica stands to the edge of the church, watching them coyly and innocently flirting with the Russian beauty. Hober feels more alone than usual. Lars is busy with marriage ideas and Father Dominik is gone, while Angelica is still undecided about a future with him. It seems the forest and its creatures are more reliable than any human, he thinks.

The Tatra Mountains sit quietly through the Spring, still covered in snow, steadfast. Hober takes the trail that leads to the East, the mountains always in sight. A great owl, its belly full of field mice, sits on the branch like Hober did as a child as Hober observes, listening, growing familiar with the paths and directions in which the sun sets. A woodpecker hammers away at the same tree. Hober spots a reliable berry bush, just in case he runs out of food. *Does he ever make a home?* he wonders. *He has pecked away at the same tree since I can remember. Perhaps making a home isn't his priority, but keeping busy is.*

Hober recalls the rules of village life, to take care of each other with absolutely no idle time. That is for the wicked and lazy!

The stars never seem to change locations in the sky, no matter where he sits in the forest. They appear in the exact same spots, night after night, though in truth they are always changing, which Hober will eventually notice.

At long last, Hober makes a permanent home. A dwelling, really. He makes it of flat boards from the mill. The small dwelling contains an iron stove fed by the wood surrounding him, along with a cot and nightstand Hober made himself. On the stand is a prayer book Father Dominik gave Hober before he left for Great Britain, along with a small porcelain bowl and one tin of beans to use in emergency if the berries shrivel or are plucked by ravens. He usually feeds off the berries and nuts of the forest, good enough for any outdoorsman. He bakes his own bread and fills it with wild berries and walnuts, stealing them away after they drop to the forest floor. Hanging on the wall are items he bought from the war surplus shop in the neighboring village. Finally, he owns a few things.

Summer arrives early. It is gratefully welcomed, the season of peeling open the tundra flowers, lured by the high sun. Blossoming blackberry bushes and river birch all seem to turn green at once. The mountains remain quiet, *too* quiet, Hober thinks. Villagers busily work and already begin storing away supplies for the next winter. The church bells chime every half hour during the week to remind the fieldworkers of their mealtimes.

While hiking, Hober discovers a prisoner of war camp. It is much smaller than he'd imagined one to be, a place where cruel men hid their acts of hatred. The camp is outlined in barbed wire, the same prickly wire he'd dreamed about, cloth hanging from it as though it were a laundry line. A rusted old tank sits heavy to the damp soil, a tattered German flag still flying from the turret. Large Xs of iron crosses called "Hedgehogs" surround the perimeter, not the same as the sweet, innocent deer Hober has always watched as they meandered in and out of hedgerows. The crosses lie defiantly to their sides as if to say, "Keep out!" or "Keep in", Hober thought.

A few pre-dug graves lay empty, intended for those who either died and were not buried, perhaps set on fire. The holes are halfway full of the rain that has ignited the rest of the forest growth. To the left is a storage shed, unsnug planks of wood holding people in, the planks so far apart you could see straight through them. A skeletal form of a Hubelwagen, a bucket car, is half-shattered from winter's cold. The sight brings a slight joy. The enemy had a hard time in the forest, he thinks. "I would never wish hardship onto another, yet this feels so terribly horrid, this place of captivity," he adds out loud.

He hears a sharp sound. The sound of pain. Walking further into the camp, he finds a rabbit stuck to barbed wire. He carefully pulls the twisted barb from the rabbit. One free, it runs and keeps running. "War is ugly; there are never winners at war!" Hober says, repeating something his father used to say.

Hober scans the camp, which is more of a conscientious objector's camp than for prisoners of war. It only held a select few who refused to fight for any side; killing wasn't in them. The men were held captive with a handful of Polish and Hungarian women, who did nothing wrong but refuse as well. In their case, they refused to be placed in makeshift brothels for German soldiers. They had families and husbands missing them terribly and waiting for them at home.

He makes its way inside the officers' barracks and notices an odd lamp. As he walks closer, he can see the stitch work on the lampshade... *flesh*. Not animal, but human. His knees buckle and he feels ill. The lampshade is stretched over a wire as the light bulb underneath illuminates the pores of the poor soul who once wore that skin, now stretched and seemingly of fabric or material. He looks about the barracks, finding human teeth with gold fillings laying in a clay bowl. Stacked atop those are more teeth.

The graves outside give Hober a better understanding of war and death. His family's deaths were one thing; they were taken by nature and a terrible mistake. These people, though, were brutally tortured, treated as if they were beneath animals. What soulless human could be so disconnected from the Lord to do such things? He wonders.

He feels the sensation once more. Loneliness steps on his shoulders and pushes him into the ground. He begins to cry, hugging the soil, moving it about with his palms. He sobs for hours, sitting in his pain as a songbird angelically twills from the highest branches. Yet, the camp is a dream of horror. No one would do such things to other humans!

He makes camp within the camp. Ghostly winds swirl about. Hober can sense the lost people's spirits, the women who died for no reason other than to protect their honor, the men born as non-fighters on borders holding no allegiance to either side, killed by the very people forcing them to kill! The camp is quiet, no crying out for family by name, no men to chop the wood to keep the Germans warm. It lies numb to the pain it once felt, a healing beginning to take place in the forest. The camp is now an empty hellscape amidst a beautiful place. A few stray animals of the forest exploring the wooden rooms, making their own bedding from old camp supplies. Nature only takes what it needs.

Hober pictures all of this as darkness drops like a movie screen, a brook trickling in the background, the same brook he played in as a child. The brook that nourished the village, that fed it melted snow, that supplied Hoslava's water, since the village had no cistern or well. Now it carries blood, a brook of red.

Hober beds down and looks up to the clarity of the sky and stars. He glances back to the sheds that held the people, imagining the horror in their eyes, their downcast hearts filled with fear. Earlier, he found a note from one of the women to her husband:

Dear Love,

I will not return, this is for certain. I am held captive by the Germans. They use us for pleasure. I look upward to the sky and picture your face when we first met, and our children and Hungary. I will miss you. I will miss holding you. One day, when you are old and are done with life, we will meet again, and I will hold you in such an embrace. God will have to push me out of the way to get a good look at you!"

Your Swinska

Hober folds the note neatly in a square and throws it into a fire he has built from wood he found on the edge of the forest. The square represents in his mind one of the squares of the unity blankets village women sewed during the war. The blue flame takes the note; the ash drifts upward to the stars. He imagines the woman's husband receiving it.

He falls into a deep sleep, even surrounded by ghosts

that are about the camp. A pair of German boots even rests at the edge of his bed. He could have very well slept in the barracks but prefers the simple honesty of the outdoors. An owl flutters by, resting on the branch overlooking him while he sleeps. Another branch snaps, and bugs land on Hober's face. He stirs but is too tired to swat them away.

The sky is wide, scooping up the dead and their souls to rest on the clouds, the crimes of war hidden away in the forest, never to be read about in history books, the people forever unnoticed.

The next morning, Hober packs up early, eats a few berries and carries along a few tins of food he finds in the camp. He walks slowly out, wondering where the people were who dug the empty graves. What happened to them? What led to their demise? Did they escape? In his heart of hearts, Hober knows the answer... a large bottle of gas with skull and crossbones on the label, poisonous gas sits nearby. "Warning! Do not inhale or digest, poisonous liquid," the bottle stated in German.

Years back, a friend from Germany came to the village to visit his aunt. The soldiers were known for their great skill at pyres, burning body atop of body, leaving the human ash behind for the wind to blow into the mountains. The valleys kept their secrets from the mountains.

He stumbles over fallen logs. Pine boughs swipe him in the face as tears fall down his cheek, his boots creating a hollow sound. He wants so much to be near Angelica, to hear her sweet voice and teasing opinions.

Suddenly, he can't reach the village fast enough!

Church bells chime at nine a.m. as the farmers make their way to the fields and the cows let loose gentle yawns.

He sees Angelica hanging white linens on the line underneath a wide, clear sky, a good day for drying clothes. He sneaks up on her, cupping her hands over her eyes. She lets out a high-pitched scream, causing Hober to laugh loudly, though she is a bit annoyed.

"Why are you so obnoxious today, Hober? Really it's too early!"

Hober puts his hand to chin, his signature look. "I was merely trying to make you laugh, Angelica... oh my!" A bit of sarcasm joins his words. "Can we just smile and laugh? I have seen something terrible, not far from here... something terrible took place and we had not the slightest clue!"

"What, Hober? What are you... what are you fabricating?"

"It's not a fabrication," he says strongly. "I saw it right out there near the brook. It's real and people died close to this village – prisoners of war!"

The look on Angelica's face could not be more serious.

"Where, Hober? Where?"

"I told you, out there near the brook. Aren't you listening to me?"

"Yes, Hober, I am listening. Let's go see it, shall we?" She is so reasonable she needs to eyewitness things for herself to truly believe the mischief of the boys.

Hober grabs her arm and pulls her to the edge of the garden. "Look, Angelica, how and why would I make up such a thing? Just come see!"

"Okay, okay, Hober. Relax. I will go with you to see this camp. Just give me a moment to hang the clothes."

Soon, Angelica finishes hanging the linens. She throws a shawl over her shoulders, a white-laced shawl with a striped pink and beige pattern, hand-stitched by her dear grandmother, who like all Polish grandmothers is known as Babka.

They set out for the forest, Hober's heart nearly beating out of his chest. His anxiety gets the better of him as they approach the clearing. Angelica also makes it known her heart is beating hard and loud. "Hober?" she whispers.

"You don't have to whisper – no one here but souls," he replies.

The forest looks different. Maybe it's the earlier time of day, or now knowing what it contains. They enter the opening near the brook and see the outbuildings, German soldiers' barracks, pits dug as graves, and the Hedgehog iron crosses laying on their sides. Angelica is speechless; she has nothing to say to Hober after accusing him of being "up to something."

"I told you!" Hober exclaims. "Here it is and we all never knew these people were here suffering. Our village is just there, through the clearing. It disgusts me we did nothing!"

"Hober, how could we have helped? We didn't know this was here! I don't know anyone in the village who came down this path." There was anger in her voice.

The buildings stand stone-faced as Hober wishes for some sign a life, a survivor. However, this camp swallowed its captives. The teeth remain in the bowl, the human lampshade now housing a burned-out bulb.

Angelica looks around the buildings and graves. The panoramic view is overwhelming; too much terror. She can feel it inside. She can feel the women, the suffering of each... oh, the feeling! "Hober, what now?" she asks. "Where are they? Where are the people?"

"Dead, Angelica. Dead!" She begins to cry. "There is more, Angelica. Come see!" Hober holds her hand as they walk into the barracks and see the lampshades and teeth. Then Hober notices some things he didn't see the first time – a pile of clothing, bits and pieces of watches, a handbag with black beaded pearls. They lay in place as if the owners would be returning to collect them. "Sickening… this is too much, Hober. I want to leave – and leave now!" Her pitch is higher than earlier.

"No, not yet. Let's see what else we can find, and we will report this to the proper authorities," Hober says.

"Who will care about a few Polish and Hungarian people? No one with a grip on reality. War doesn't care about these people any longer.

Hober realizes Angelica is making sense in some of what she says. "Okay, then let's at least bury their things in the graves they dug," he suggests.

"Where are their bodies, Hober? Why can't we bury *them*?"

"They are ash and already in heaven, Angelica. Let's just bury their things so no one and come out here and take them, okay?"

"Okay." She whispers out of respect.

They bury the people's items in the empty graves, a few still filled with rain. It leaves them with a sense of closure; no one can take anything else away from them again.

Later, Hober tells a few elders about the camp. The elders inspect the camp and pull down the barbed wire, so animals and humans won't be hurt by the pricks of war. They decide to leave everything else as is, a memorial for those silenced in the forest. Hober already knows he will never forget this experience, this face-to-face with death itself.

The end of war is never easy. Massive groups wander the tundra, refugees from other villages burned and cities bombed. This results in more homeless people than the land can support. The only help will come from the Red Cross, once they can make their way to the rural areas.

Overseeing all this tragedy are the mountains. They stand like saints watching over their people, mountains that never flinch in their steadfastness, even during a bombing. They are there always, and always will be.

In the village, former prisoners liberated from the camps pass by, starving so much they clutch onto single potatoes. The villagers hand out milk, while they give the orphaned children loaves of bread. Hober's heart aches for the dirty-faced small children that worked the factories under cruel conditions as they watched the smoke of incinerated human bodies drift and twist into the clouds like kites.

Night comes again. Spring is with the land, as bright green leaves fill the trees, the seedlings of future nuts forming and growing into chestnuts. Hober loves the clean, crisp smell of the air. Father Dominik writes Hober, telling him about the big change to his spiritual work: he is now a bishop of the church.

Meanwhile, Lars decides to travel to Krakow to help rebuild the city. He is also going to give private violin lessons. Lars has become quite the violinist over the years, something for which is mother is very happy. Funny, how life on the tundra grows its children into balanced adults, each carrying a deeply personal story of survival, perseverance, and the desire to be really good at what they do.

At the church, Hober slowly befriends the new priest, Father Miesko, who is even younger than Hober. He wants to give Father Miesko what was given to him, when he was alone: the support and gift of friendship.

He hears music from the town hall where the villagers meet weekly, the tranquil strokes of a violin giving him a sense of calm. His future is undecided, and time is not always a friend. But he never forgot his promise to himself – to give back to the world what it tried to give him during the war.

A new family arrives in the village, a German couple with a daughter, Frieda. Hober watches them carefully move their belongings into a tiny house on one of the lanes, a house that rests nearly across the street from the church. He is a bit cynical after seeing a prisoner of war camp firsthand. Are these truly kind and good people? Their belongings are frugal, their clothes a bit tattered and worn. At the least, they've been impacted by the war. Hober also notices Frieda's beauty, her blonde hair that flows down to her mid-back and her petite stature. He will keep observing them for a few days before giving them a proper greeting, now very reluctant about strangers in the village. Their arrival brings up the old stories of his *dziadek* (grandfather) settling in the village long ago.

Nature is the great teacher to the tundra, whether in offering signs of approaching storms, heavy drought that summer can create, or the way the mountains change light into dancing hues of purple. All of it beneath the night sky and brilliant show of stars that bring along the next day. The turning over of a leaf signifies a thunderstorm, which appear so clearly on the flat terrain before the land reaches the mountains.

Chapter Five

The seasons change quickly. Life sweeps into a fast pace to prepare for winter, which is a taker of sunlight and warmth, but also a giver of rest.

The villagers go about their day. Hober sits occasionally on the branch that overhung their family home, daydreaming of his mother baking in the Spring kitchen with the window opened wide. Early breezes sweep the house of the scent of poppy seed bread in the oven, along with the warmth the house held, with or without occupants. He still feels the sense of loss daily, let love is a prospect he begins to desire, having a family of his own one day. He already feels love for the tundra, the echoing cry of wolves, that "wild at heart" feeling when he has a true kinship with all things living in the forest.

The mountains seem to call to Hober. He wonders what lies over them, places like the Ukraine, Soviet Ukraine, a forbidden place. He takes in the stories of lost soldiers making their way back home, telling of the horrors of life and war, of living under a tyrannical regime. He once knew a young Ukrainian, who went to school with Hober when the school still had funds to keep it running. It closed midway through the year when he was eleven. When that happened, his mother's duties increased and gained even more purpose; she taught Hober and the other children about the larger world, languages, the people. He feels an itch, the itch of belonging to something larger than village life.

Hober's friends sprout and disperse in different directions, each trying their best to be successful adults. He grows close to Father Miesko, who gently yet firmly guides him with questions about his expectations in life, which city to live in, and others. He does it to form a more rounded person. Hober reads letters from Father Dominik on London city life, and envies the possibilities it holds. Warsaw seems to be a beacon for the lost and wayward who hold similar hopes, which ignites his desire to leave the village for better opportunities. He has nothing to keep him in the village, and it doesn't seem like Angelica feels the same way about him as he does about her. He feels like a lost puppy, trying to find his way. His faith lends him the gift in believing in himself, yet even as he continues growing into a man, he is naïve on life outside the village.

While contemplating all of it, he runs into a village elder. "Bentz, can you give me an answer on what I should do now with my life?" he asks. "As you know, my family has gone and it's just me and the forest. As I know, the forest can only lend an ear, never any words of advice."

"Dear Hober, you must always be aware that the world outside village life is not comparable to here. This will be something you have to experience, and that will give you the knowledge that you're asking me for." Bentz knew it was up to Hober to decide his own future.

Hober feels each impression in the tundra, each war scar imprinted on the land. The empty war camp is a place he will never forget, nor want to remove from his mind. Those images will remain alive in his thoughts. He honors those who suffered and did the best they could to survive, the graves dug by their own hands, the clothing piled as if leaves of autumn waiting to be burned and discarded. The images humble him each day. So does something else: *the Germans were so close to our village, yet left the village untouched.* He sees the blessing in its great disguise of angst.

He reflects on Bentz's words while recalling his mother's story of how he was born. His birth took many hours on the cold, heavy winter night. His mother's pride in him was obvious from the moment he was born, a special human being she would sadly have to let go of, all too soon. In a sense, her death saved her from the painful separation of seeing her son go into his adult life.

Hober also weighs the pros and cons of leaving the village and forest in which he has spent a life in which he witnessed the death of his entire family, lived through droughts, survived winters. He has loved many and lost many, on the trains that departed and took neighbors to places he'd never heard of... never to hear from the neighbors again. Through it all, his mother gave him the gift of the world around him, of knowing each surrounding country and where it lay on the globe. He uses the knowledge to appear worldly. Once he leaves the village and begins mingling with city people, he does not want to seem an uneducated kid from the countryside.

He sees Grandmother Helena sitting and watching the other villagers hard at work, spiking plants and dead-heading sunflowers. She waves and motions him over.

"Hello, young man," she says, a smile on her face. "Have a seat. Let's do some talking, and after we talk, I will get you something to eat. I can see your ribs... and only people who are dire show their ribs!" Helena is an elder with a tongue that says exactly what she wills.

Hober is taken aback by her generosity. She always appears angry or grumpy or selfish. Now he realizes he is wrong; so are the village kids.

"Thank you, Helena, I would love to have a sit with you," he says. "I am just wandering about, trying my best to sort out life. I am old enough now to leave the village yet torn at the same time. I will miss the beauty of the tundra and the mountains' echoes, and the villagers, too."

Helena begins to laugh. "Hober, dear boy, this village has been here for centuries and as far as I can tell, it will be here for centuries more. Go live your life and experience it like a philosopher, see things, hear things – and live it!" Helena shuffles inside to fetch a paczki – a Lenten donut. She makes them by the hundreds to share with the villagers.

Her tone startles Hober; it's so matter-of-fact, as if she has lived somewhere else, maybe in another time. He takes her advice and keeps stores with the voice of Father Miesko and his friends. Perhaps it is time to leave.

Spring feels as if it comes earlier than the lowlands. The mountains reflect the sun, the crops grow more mature, and sunflowers and lilies of the valley dot the terrain.

Helena returns with the paczki. "Hober, this is your life. Live it and live it full! This place will always be here. Now please, I want you to stay the night. I am tired of seeing you wander around like a stray. I have plenty of room; stay for as long as you need to decide on leaving. You need a good place to rest before your journey begins.

Flabbergasted, Hober politely accepts her offer.

Helena is known by the church to not be very generous, so Hober has caught her on a good day. He takes his things inside and she fixes him a cup of tea. The sky rolls into night on this, the first time since his family's death he has felt a firm, safe roof over his head with the promise he will stay under the same roof the next night, too.

After falling asleep, he dreams of the camp, the death camp held secret, the mystery and the men who ran the camp, heartless men. His dreams flit in and out of the tundra, the great wolf and bear out there, the barbed wire that harms and terrorizes innocence. His dreams feel like more than dreams... they feel like reflections of his life.

By dusk his dreams lead him to the rimless lake he so loves, the hawk that flies above with vision so spectacular he wishes he had it as well. He will miss the scents of freshly cut wood, the timbers floating in the pool waiting to soften enough to bend into eaves for a roof.

When he comes out to the kitchen, Helena has breakfast cooking on the stove. She stuffs the belly of the stove with fresh-cut wood; the smell drifts to Hober like a ghost. His eyes begin to water. "Hober, place this in your mind," Helena says. "The village will always be here, and it will wait for you!"

He settles down enough to eat the dumplings floating in warm milk, along with the extra sugar treat Helena spreads over the dumplings. Sugar and salt are luxuries in any war.

Hober does appreciate Helena's bluntness. It shows she cares – and he needs all the caring he can find.

After breakfast, he packs his knapsack for a day trek to weigh out his future. The forest can give the exact answer he is searching for, he believes. Even with Helena's rigid yet true advice, he needs one more sign-off, so he heads to the forest, the place he knows best out of all the villagers.

Nearby, a train whistle blows; Hober skips a step, the whistle breaking his concentration. "No worries," he says to himself out loud. "I have no bindings here. The train comes and goes weekly. Why do I feel a rush to find an answer?"

He walks through the butter yellow daisies. The wind kicks up and dies down, tickling his face. He gives the sun a smile. He still resembles a child in ways; perhaps the fire took away something and left him with something else, a perpetual child inside a growing man. He has great intent on making an impression, though, achieving something others have not.

He walks the tundra on old paths, half-buried under grasses and weeds. The mountains sit quietly, the air electrified with static, a storm swirling about. Black clouds accumulate, removing the blue sky as Hober walks a bit faster for shelter inside a small cave, one unoccupied by the great bear. He knows it is safe to ride out the storm there. As he enters, his eyes adjust to the dim light of the cave.

The storm cuts loose, trees cracking and swaying outside. It appears to be a long storm, so Hober finds a few branches near the entrance before the rain can soak them. He makes a firepit; the ensuing fire lights up the entire cave. He notices old Russian symbols on the walls, messages from travelers of centuries ago making their way south. "I wonder how many have stayed in this cave?" he asks aloud as he pokes the fire.

The feeling of loneliness comes over Hober as hours go by, making him bored of the rain. While waiting for it to end, he makes his way further into the cave. The fire light now sprinkles toward the rear, where he finds a skeleton. His hands begin to shake. It's another soldier... one who came to the village on his way back home... His heart practically stops.

It's Fritz, the German soldier he talked to. His face remains on the skeletal frame as if on purpose, nature devouring his lower body while leaving his face frozen, glazed eyes pointed to the ceiling. He feels pangs of anxiety, feelings he'd never had before, too much death for a young person. He bends down, grabs a small wipe cloth from his knapsack, and places it on the boy soldier's face, feeling so much remorse for this stranger he didn't know.

He stands for a few minutes, looking at the belongings the soldier carried: a shiny knife with a skull on the shank, the S.S. hat still on his head; no doubt he was proud to be in such a branch of the German military. He didn't notice the hat when Fritz walked through camp; now it sits on his head like a beacon of murder. Disgusted, Hober kicks the soil by the soldier's feet, angry at the possibilities of what the German had done.

He walks back to the fire and waits out the storm, every so often turning and frowning at the dead soldier boy.

Finally, the rain ends. The storm gave Hober plenty of time to decide: he will leave the village. City life is now his future.

He walks out of the forest with a sense of accomplishment. As he returns to Helena's home, she can see in his face and eyes that he has decided to leave. *I am going.* His lips didn't have to form the words.

Hober bids farewell to those he has grown to love. This love is dear, something he will never take for granted. His love for Angelica, on the other hand, will always just be; he knows she will never be his, yet the love is steadfast in his heart. Lars is well along in his life, as is Father Dominick, while Father Miesko has become a dear friend.

He carefully chooses the correct words. "Father Miesko, kind friend, you have lent a hand to my loneliness, and for that, I will never forget you. I leave tomorrow for Warsaw, needing to learn about the world. Here in the village, I feel like I am suffocating."

"Hober, I truly understand and give you my blessings. If you need me, all you have to do is pray and I will be there with you in spirit." Father Miesko always seems to speak with gentle undertones. Hober finds him very tranquil, and his calmness reassures him that he is doing the right thing.

The day seems a bit odd; his sense of the unknown rises. He will miss his mountains as they will miss him. He will truly miss the echoing of an early avalanche and the blooming of Spring on the tundra.

The summer ends abruptly. Seemingly all at once, the trees turn golden and the apples full, the air releasing the sharp scents of Autumn. Leaves drift like the upcoming snows. He prepares for his departure by walking to the church to light one more candle. He kneels and prays for the village and his safe journey.

The whistle blows. The five-car train departs from the small station made of thin slatted pine. The station master waves to the passengers, and off goes the train. Hober is excited about his prospects and imagines what the grand city of Warsaw will look like. The train sways like a full-bellied cow, which comforts him.

The countryside is dotted in small villages and rolling wheat fields, grain and hay tucked into bales like scarves on a cold winter day. The steaming cup of tea sitting beneath the passenger next to Hober entices his sense of what is ahead in the cafes: musicians playing flutes and violin, shop windows laced in nothing but perfection. He truly cannot believe he has left the village; his memories of family already cling tighter to his heart. Family is the most important treasure any man can hope for.

The train click clacks, crossing dusty roads, farmers watching from their carts pulled by heavy bulls. A man's day in Poland begins before the sun, and rest only comes when the sun is no longer.

The journey takes a day and a half, leaving Hober a bit weary. The noises start to add up: the whistle blowing noisily as the train crosses over every single dirt road and into villages, the snoring sounds of the elderly man wearing a box-shaped hat, his jacket of chevrons a bit tattered. Hober focuses on his imagination of what city life must be, a place of newly birthed hopes, even after the devastation of European cities levied by the war.

Finally, the train arrives. Disheveled passengers disembark as chaos flocks into Warsaw station, mixed with the disruptive cries from people wanting out. Hober is confused; wasn't Warsaw a place of refuge and better economic opportunities? Instead, he finds devastation, a Warsaw tired and broken, the people dirty and unpolished. The train station resembles a makeshift hospital with crutches and bandages lying on the maroon tiles. The "Phoenix City", Warsaw, has survived many wars, including this last, when some unfortunates tried to survive in the ghettos. Even Rome could not avoid the grasp of Hitler and his long arm of atrocities. It all leaves Hober in deep shock. This is not what he aspired Warsaw to be.

He makes his way to the streets. He sees quickly how all the bombing stripped a bold city bare and brought it to its knees. He quickly remembers his mother reading histories of the world's great cities to him. The Baroque, Rococo and neoclassical architecture that defined majestic Warsaw's skyline before the war, some buildings dating back seven centuries, now resembles a jigsaw puzzle. The Soviets rummage through the last standing houses. The Bohemian Warsaw for which he traveled far now lays in ruins.

Warsaw looks as sad as the tragedy that befell it. The Red Army has posted statistics on how many Poles died in the city; the number is between 150,000 and 200,000, not including the Jewish people from the ghettoes that imprisoned them. When the war began, Hober recalls from his reading, there were 350,000 Jews in Warsaw. The Nazi troops took those civilians into Germany, placing them in POW camps as the Soviets liberated the Warsaw suburbs.

Hober stumbles over bricks and street lamps that have fallen to the ground. A small child approaches him, begging for coins. He has very little to give, yet he reaches into his pocket and pulls out enough for a loaf of freshly baked bread. The little child takes the money and runs, frightened of him. The world seems so frightened now, even by a leaf skirting above one's head. The bombings unnerved everyone. It strikes Hober that he will never find his friends, nor will this place hold his future. "How did I come to be in such a lie?" he asks himself out loud.

Back to the countryside. His thoughts travel back to the countryside.

Hober makes a left hand turn into a dire-looking street. Linens and clothing are strewn on the ground as if a riot took place; remnants of human life flow into the gutters. It is quiet, too quiet. Where is the life? Hober grows fearful. The ghetto has died; no one moves from the buildings, nor is anyone walking the streets. Star of David armbands lie in piles near empty baskets that once held breads; off to the side, a single shoe waits for its owner to return. The smell is deep and dank, sewage cluttering the once fresh water in the sheds and barrels. Nothing exists any more, not even a free-flying bird. "Death only remains for such a place," Hober says, his voice notched with fear and anger. How could any human do these things to another human?

He thinks of what he packed in his knapsack. There are acorns from the forest, which remind him of freedom. He carries a few eggs, a reminder of life, along with his notebook filled with sketches of the mountains, holding his dreams of finding a mountain pass to the Ukraine. So many families want to be with other family members, he thinks, yet the mountains too become like an army, holding people back.

He prays under his breath. Nothing good can come of Warsaw until its face is lifted once again.

Hober also has heard the next largest city, Krakow, is still locked in the pulse of the war. Many of its citizens were shipped to the city for extermination; the railway cars are stained with sweat and tears. He finds life oddly too real. Death walks just as life does, sometimes pushed into an early grave. He writes in his notebook, the pages dirty from travel, a mark added from the juicy apple he is eating. A drop of life, the seed of life, spreads onto a page of sketches and words. He longs for home, the safety of the tundra, the happy yellow flowers and sunsets of summer swirling in pink.

He decides to return to Hoslava, but not to take the train

home. He collects a number of homeless people, the survivors, promising them a sweeter life with hard work and the sense of knowing exactly who they can become. He thinks back to the time he met the German soldier making his way back home, the dirt on his face, his belongings worn thin. Time changes everything except what is most important.

Chapter Six

Hober finds the people tired and distraught, their legs still shaking from war, their hearts emptied by numbness. "Come with me," he says. "I am returning home to my village. Come with me and let's all start over."

A young girl in her teens walks up. She looks Hober in the eyes. "Why? Why do you care about us?" she asks. "How do we know that you won't take us to post-war camps? I have heard of places where those who are homeless are forced to go!"

The accusation annoys Hober at first, but he understands. "I am Polish, too," he says softly. "I'm sorry that my village had no idea of the magnitude of this war. I too am a victim of loss and I am here only to help."

The young girl begins to cry. "I have no one left. They are all in camps, waiting to be liberated."

Hober realizes she has no idea of what he knows from finding the camp near the village: the crematoriums and human experiments; work so hard in the labor camps it killed many. She tells him she believes such stories to be propaganda meant to turn everyone against the strong German army.

That leaves him disgusted. "Stay here then! Just stay and wait for your precious Germans to lend you a hand. All you will get is a life of prostitution and then being tossed away."

His memory comes back, fresh. It never fails him. He is back in the forest, at the hidden concentration camp, the teeth in a small pile on an S.S. officer's nightstand, empty vodka bottles and signs of meat purchased by monies taken from the women. He thinks of the graves dug and never filled, not knowing the fate of the people in the camp. He pictures the owl overseeing all that took place in the death camp.

Night falls with a bit of early autumn chill. The people collect wood as a caravan of gypsies bumps past them, their wares chiming like little bells. They disappear into the night.

The fire illuminates the faces of the lost as Hober takes a head count. "Dusan, I will call you 'number one'. Vladislav, I will call you 'number two'. Elena, I will call you 'number three,'" he says.

The girl with whom he argued is next. "I will call you 'number four'—"

"My name is not number four, it is MIRIAM!" She screams out the Jewish name given her by the Rabbi. "I will no longer hide who I am. I am not a Christian. I am Jewish!" she proclaims.

To her surprise, Hober holds her arm in full understanding. "I don't want you to be anything that you are not," he says. "Miriam it is; Miriam is what I will call you. The others have names of Serbian descent, so in order to be organized, I must know them as a number."

Miriam agrees. "We were given numbers at the beginning of this war. The others who are not Jewish hold numbers, too, for they are orphans and came from orphanage camps. But now we no longer need numbers."

"I *will* keep my number system, for surely we will pick up others along the way," Hober barks back, his patience wearing thin.

Above, the night sky blackens, as if colored in ink. Wide and starlit as ever, the night resembles Warsaw and the emptiness it holds.

The five journeyers gather leaves and lay down the leaves keeping the dampness from their clothing. There is no food. Gypsies are known for their storage of food, yet the nearby group offers none to the young band of travelers. Hober's stomach growls. He would give anything for a bowl of dumplings. The eggs ran out days ago. There is no bread or milk, just dirty faces gazing upward.

An early snow begins falling, lacing several tall pine trees in white. It makes Hober miss home more than ever. Later, several more people make their way to the sleeping area Hober and his companions have set up. He invites them to stay. There is no food, but the warm fire keeps them comfortable through the night.

The sky clears. Light from the stars twinkles and brightens the area like flares. Hober counts the clearest stars... one, two, three, four, five, six – the exact number of people now in his care. He takes it as a significant sign. Six to care for, six to keep safe on the journey back.

The village has grown from the births of summer babies, all blessed by Father Miesko. What will be a problem with adding six more mouths to feed? Hober thinks. He doesn't care. He will find a way, even if that means placing his companions in the abandoned prisoner of war camp. After he cleans it out, the nearby lake will offer food, and shelter will be beneath the roofs of those who were taken away.

The night grows long, too long for tired feet and spirits. Hober tries his best to stay positive, knowing life in the village made him who he is. He knows it will give these refugees a better start than where they came from.

Morning arrives with a songbird chirping on a nearby branch. As he opens his eyes, the first beams of sunlight seem to be guiding his eyes to the right of the field where they camped. It is cluttered with tanks and decaying corpses. Hober finds it curious that the scent isn't obvious; perhaps the shifting winds carried the horror with them.

The day begins. He gathers the refugees and snuffs the fire out with the toe of his boot. Miriam yawns and stretches as she begins to complain about her sore feet and back. "Miriam, this day will feel long enough without your complaining," Hober says, a stern tone to his voice. She tucks her scarf into a pocket and brushes her hair with her fingers; her thick locks shine under the sun. She is alert and sharp, yet seems innocent in many ways, he thinks.

They begin to walk along the train tracks, and come across a young boy about seven, Hober guesses. Smudges of dirt cover the boy's face where tears ran the day before. His face is so dirty it is hard to make out his facial features. He looks Arabic or of some Middle Eastern descent. He wears a red scarf around his neck and in his palm, carries a red string with tiny bells attached.

"What are those for?" Hober asks.

"They were my brother's," the boy says, his dialect almost unrecognizable. "They belonged to his goats. Now he has died and the goats, too, and all I have left are these bells."

Remorse fills Hober's heart. Remorse for the boy's dilemma. "What can I call you, little dirty boy?" he asks.

"I am not dirty!" he screams. "I had to hide from the Nazis... or I think they were Nazis! My family has died, and

I have no one."

Hober picks and hauls him up with one arm, the other picking a small leaf from the tree for him. "I want you to take care of this leaf," Hober says. "Keep it in your pocket, for the leaf has made its way from summer's droughts into autumn's winds. It is a treasure, just like you are."

The boy holds and inspects the leaf, then gently slides it into his pocket. "What is your name?" Hober asks again.

"Tallal."

"Tallal? Well then, okay Tallal, let's get walking! You can stay with us, and no more worries about the Nazis; they no longer exist." Hober says it with some hesitation, since he truly does not know where all the Nazis have gone. Will they cross paths with the retreating, notorious man-killing machine? He has no idea.

The little boy holds Hober's hand for the first hour of the journey as the group, now eight in number, walk towards the east. Hober looks over at him and marvels at his striking black hair and light green eyes that have already seen way too much. Gypsies journey past every so often, clanking tins from hooks on the side of the caravans, the horses letting out sputters, their hooves grinding into the dry soil. They carry on, as if the band of young people is invisible. It angers Hober; after all, where did the gypsies themselves come from? Romania? Lithuania? All were refugees, too, searching for better lives. *Why not toss us some bread or eggs?* But gypsies were used to their own persecutions from others, too, and learned to mind their own business in a dog-eat-dog world.

As morning shifts to afternoon, those with tired feet and hungry bellies begin to complain. Almost all of them. "That's enough! I can't take any more. I don't know what do to feed you!" an exasperated Hober finally exclaims to his band of youths. "Leave me alone and be quiet."

A village comes into view. It looks intact as far as he can see. They walk up to the village's name sign, which has graffiti written across it in red letters: "Kill the Germans." The sign angers him; he's had enough with death. *What killers humans sometimes are*, he thinks.

They approach the village slowly. A few chickens waddle around the street as linens dry in the autumn sign. Hober looks around. No signs of people. It unnerves him.

A small dog runs to his feet, barking intently, looking like it wants Hober to follow. Hober obliges and follows the dog to a shed; inside, he finds a litter of new pups. As joy enters his heart, he leans down to wrap the puppies in a small piece of cloth, the cloth that has been holding his father's crucifix. The puppies become quiet and content. He leaves the shed, still uneasy. *Where are all the people?* The doors to the homes are wide open, smoke lofting from chimneys...

He walks toward the back of the village and finds a garden wall of wooden crossbars lying half on the ground, as if turbulence took down the wall. At the far end of the garden, he sees bodies stacked upon each other like morning cakes. Human bodies, their dresses covered in dirt and blood. All women! No doubt the men were taken off to war camps by Germans that paid no mind to the war ending. They were like boxers in the ring, not wanted to end the fight even though they were all punched out.

Hober turns back to his fellow travelers. He walks swiftly and soberly straight ahead, focused on the seven faces waiting for hm. Tallal, the youngest, wears fear on his face.

Hober gathers him again into his arms. "It is time to leave here," he says to the others.

The task of taking them into the village is much harder than he imagined, but they have no food and very little water. As the day shifts into early evening, they walk past untended fields, picking through rotten vegetables, hoping to find something good enough to eat. Miriam begins to cry along with Dusan and Elena, numbers one and three in Hober's personal memory chart. But he had another reason for calling them by number; attachments come with names. He was guarding himself after feeling the loss of love too many times already. His belly growls again. He realizes nature is the greatest teacher and provider and that it will provide for them somehow.

Finally, they come across a field of ripe tomatoes ready to burst open. Too bad there is no bread to squeeze these wonderful tomatoes onto, he thinks. He remembers Easter, the foods places on lacy family tablecloths, eggs cracked by each person sitting at the table, playing "which egg wins?", then eating. The full belly sensation comes back as he rests by the fire and his mother sings.

Now, he has no idea what to do. "Let's just gather the tomatoes and put them in your pockets and scarves," he says.

Tallal squashes a few by holding them too hard as the juices run down his arms and legs. The sight takes Hober back to the blood of war. "Toss the tomatoes to the ground," he says. Tallal does that.

Behind them, Miriam has stopped walking. She throws herself to the ground, causing a fit amongst the others. Then they fall to the ground and refuse to get back up. "Get up, you brats!" Hober says. "Get up and stop it right now. We are nearly there, just a little bit past this tomato field, just hang on!"

Vladislav – number two, Hober notes – gets up from the ground, wiping himself clean and stuffing a tomato into his pocket. "Okay, Hober, let's go!" he says. Hober likes his steady voice, his spirit of endurance. The others follow Vladislav's example, getting up and cleaning themselves off. They resume walking.

After night falls, Hober thinks of how much longer the return walk is than the train ride to Warsaw. Soon, it is pitch black. Nothing can be seen, not even their hands in front of them, it seems. The only sound they hear is Tallal sloppily eating a tomato. "This is better than nothing," he says. "My mother would cut tomatoes and we would eat them with flatbreads and goat cheese."

His description leads to unwelcome and now painful belly growls. "Stop, Tallal! Stop that!" Hober yells. "You are making everyone else hungry."

"I only miss my family, Hober. Do you not understand this?"

"Yes, Tallal, I do, very much so. Just stop talking altogether, okay?"

The night passes slowly, with no stars to keep them company, no wood for a fire, and no voices speaking of homes and families. As they lay under the black sky, they hear crackling twigs and the howls of distant wolves. Hober is used to such sounds, and feels again a part of nature, nature being his surrogate family. He knows the youths are frightened, so be begins to sing and mimics playing the violin, even though the others can't see him. By his final note, everyone is asleep. He lays awake all night, dutifully watching over the group.

Morning rises. Hober rubs a tomato on his jacket to wipe off the heavy frost that outlined their bodies as they slept on the ground. The tomato is cool and refreshing as he holds the image of frost outlining sleeping children along with his other memories. It dawns on him that it has been days since they've had water, a greater necessity than food.

"Get up, let's go," he says. "We are nearly at my village, and once there, we will eat well." That promise awakens everyone.

Miriam complains again about the lack of water and her sore feet. Hober decides to make an even more promising bribe. "We will have fresh water, and eggs, and dumplings, and beets, and honey, and cheeses, and comfortable beds, if only you will stop complaining, Miriam," he says. She begins to cry again.

As they begin walking, Hober whispers a few prayers for a safe journey to Saint Christopher, the patron saint of lost causes. He rubs the crucifix his father gave him. *If only I could be the man father was, taking these people to the village for a safe life,* he thinks, *I will know father heard my prayers.*

He feels like keeping to himself. The others are quiet, too, except for Tallal, who sings ancient Middle Eastern chants. Prayer time is at high noon, which Tallal knows as he watches the sun slowly arc upward in the sky.

At mid-day, a group passes. Hober examines their clothing and eyes, making sure they are safe and not bypassing soldiers still bent on killing. Four men walk past, their heads hanging low, never looking at Hober or the others... a tell-tale sign they are ashamed of something.

Hober tells the youths to do the same, not to look the men in their eyes. They do exactly as he says.

The four men still do not look their way. They shuffle past like ghosts, ghosts of what they used to be, ghost figures walking to nowhere. None wear uniforms, yet their faces tell stories of death and all the taking.

Hober and his band do not say a word for hours. He can barely think of the things those men likely did to the Poles, all guided by a lunatic named Hitler.

The seventh day of October arrived with Hober helping seven people in the small band of refugees, including seven-year-old Tallal. They have walked longer than he hoped, three days by Hober's count, and he feels he lost his sense of direction several days back. It seems they've been walking in a huge circle since, getting nowhere. He shuffles his feet, his gait no longer allowing wide, broad steps. *What if we don't make it back? What if I am responsible for the deaths of these seven?* His mind is playing tricks on him, an effect of dehydration. They need food and water, badly. The river they cross, though, is tainted with the carcasses of cows and other livestock. Now and then a human body floats past. The waters are undrinkable, a great disappointment to them.

Tallal tells the group his birthday is in a week's time. They do not respond. In ordinary circumstances, they would start thinking about a great celebration, but they have no cakes, no songs to sing. Direness joins them in their weariness.

Hober concentrates intently, making sure the next route he chooses is the correct one back to the village. He says the name of the village out loud: "Hoslava!"

Hoslava...

He knows the Tatra Mountains will guide him, and the mountain shadows will lead them to Hoslava, where the villagers will feed and protect them. "We are one!" That is the village rule. He recalls some of Father Dominik's words, which gives him the will power to move on.

One day later, the dirt road is empty. The train whistle sounds out as the tundra comes into view. Home is near now. Hober steps up a few beats, walking faster; the others can barely keep up. All seven are now dragging themselves along, which makes Hober proud of their endurance.

It begins to rain, first gently, then a pelting rain, the sort that hurts. Autumn rains bring along winter. Hober knows the villagers are preparing for the upcoming months, the season of rest after a summer of toiling and mending and harvesting.

Soon, the band of refugees becomes soaked. "Hober! Where is this village?" Miriam asks. "Is it even real? Or are you just playing a game with us?"

"No, Miriam, lay off now. I'm certainly not in a good mood, just like you. I want to be there, too." Hober realizes he does not speak this way normally. Miriam can certainly push all of his wrong buttons, the way she tries his patience.

No one in the band speaks to each other. They step in and out of puddles as the rain drips off their weary noses, Hober feeling they are long overdue in his estimated time of returning to the village.

Evening lamps sit in the front windows of each village house. Smoke from hearths fills the air. Hober throws his arms up, thrilled to be back home. They walk up to the church, which is quiet for mid-week. No evening prayers are taking place, so Hober seeks out Father Miesko, finding this a great time to ask for a favor.

He walks up to Father Miesko, who is surprised to see him. "Father, hello! How are you? I need a favor of you and I am sorry for asking such a favor after not seeing you."

Father stops his task of replacing candles and tidying up pews after the previous day's prayer hour. "Hober! I am so happy to see you! Come in…" He looks at the seven young faces, all soaked and obviously exhausted and in need of food. "….and yes, you can stay here for the night, all of you."

Hober is beyond happy to see Father Miesko. He gives him a warm hug, not something he is fine-tuned to doing, but now, he wants to hug everyone.

Father sits with the seven guests and asks questions about their journey. "Do you know how far we have walked?" Miriam asks. "Can we please talk in the morning?" None of the others speak; they are too tired to talk.

Father laughs at her bluntness. She will be something one day when she is grown, that is for certain, he thinks. Next to him, Hober rolls his eyes and winks. After tucking the refugees into the pews, tiredness overtakes him, too. They have come a long way.

The church seems odd now that he has returned. He does not see the familiar faces of Lars and Angelica, or Father Dominik. He truly likes Father Miesko, yet the people he grew up with mean so much, and now everyone is scattered into adulthood. And he has come back.

Father Miesko lights the last candle, casting the church in a gentle glow. In this light, it is hard to believe war has taken so much outside the church doors and beyond the tundra. Hober lies awake with his back against the first pew. The coolness takes him into the forest and the camp. He will never forget that sight, nor Warsaw, nor what war forever removes.

All the kids are asleep now, but Hober feels a sense of duty to keep an eye on these refugees, who trusted a complete stranger to walk them to a small village they had never heard of. He counts the ceiling beams – one, two, three, four; one, two, three, four. Four wooden beams, cut from the forest of those who go lost and missing, the forest of the great bear and the great wolf. Next to him, Tallal sleeps lightly; he, too, is trying to keep an eye on the others, sharing the sense of protecting with Hober. After his great loss, he now cares for them as if they are family.

Finally, Hober falls asleep. He dreams lucidly of the forest and Angelica, the POW camp, the clothing piled up, the teeth and human lampshades made of flesh, the empty graves. What took place there? He also dreams of the beauty of the woods and majesty of the mountains. Warsaw leaves an imprint as well, one he may one day write about after he heals in the hands of nature. But first, he wants to reacquaint himself with the woods, perhaps building a small cottage a bit closer to the foothills, a place of yellow flowers and clear wandering brooks.

Hober and Tattal awaken to the boom of thunder. Winter is approaching, and the skies have no idea which way to drift. The Eastern winds collide with the Siberian winds of the north, peeling back tiles on the church roof. A few slide onto the ground, frightening Tallal. "Don't worry. God is not angry at you for eating the last apple, the last apple we had to share once we left Warsaw," Hober says, trying to comfort him with humor.

Tallal is stunned. He had no idea Hober saw him eat the last apple. His cheeks turn rosy as he looks away.

Hober's heart is forgiving, forged that way after the runaway fires from the harvest festival that killed his family. When it happened, he blamed neither God nor nature.

Accidents take place, sadly, but the true crime of humanity is killing on purpose. The Germans sure had that down to a 'T', he thinks, Nazi soldiers who only see white and a pure race. Thankfully, the villagers are different, since the seven refugees are of several different backgrounds. He knows Tallal and the others will do fine in the village.

A crisp scent fills the morning air. Wagons filled with squash and melons pass by chestnuts and oaks glowing in their autumn dress. The entire tundra is engulfed in flames of color. "Wake up, everyone," Hober says gently. "Thanks to Father Miesko, we have food to eat!"

They wake up still tired, rubbing their eyes and yawning after the best sleep they'd had in longer than they can count. They feel safe with Hober. He leads them to the church meeting area, next to a small kitchen, where a table is set with breads, cheeses and eggs, and steaming hot tea. Soon, the smells of the food mingle with the laughter of young people eating again!

"We are so lucky!" Miriam exclaims, crying again, this time a happy cry. "We are so lucky!"

They laugh as one, slapping each other's backs. Usually the complainer, Miriam's joy is refreshing to the entire bunch. Hober watches, shaking his head. Life is sure a funny thing; the journey will impact all of them. He also knows Warsaw will one day rebuild, violins will play again, and they can return to the Phoenix City. Poets will write about the city that fell so many times over the centuries, only to stand taller after each brick was replaced and city streets filled with people again. "Unlike most cities," Hober's mom told him once, "Warsaw is not pretentious or posh or rude. It is a melting pot for those who see the finer parts of a simple life."

Father Miesko swings open the doors of the church to villagers, a subtle reminder that it is always open. While the villagers frequent the church on holidays and all of the commemorative days for saints, Father has big hopes for them to again make daily prayer a regular choice. Meanwhile, residents listen as the refugees Hober brought to town tell of what they saw and the losses of war. Those elder women of some German descent feel ashamed. But no one can blame anyone; Hitler hypnotized those who were vulnerable and dire. The people of Poland soon try their best to keep the human condition in their minds. War is ugly; to give is the only way to heal.

When the morning train arrives at the station, no one departs. Hober looks around; there are now more women than men in the village. Too many men have lost the most precious gift of all, their lives. Women in the outer villages and towns have learned how to carry on without them. The Soviets carried away many to fight in their armies. Those who refused were shipped off to camps, where they could now be found, dead or alive.

Hober leads the seven refugees from the train station to village center, where a festival begins to celebrate the end of the war. They are also celebrating the prospects of the village growing from people like these refugees, searching for life once again. Streamers of bright reds, purples and whites crisscross overhead, hanging from trees or eaves. Large barrels of cucumbers pickled to a perfect green hue float in the sweet taste of vinegar. Ruby red beets lay in clear hand-blown plates next to bowls of eggs and cheeses, and breads twisted into gorgeous knots of deliciousness. A small band plays the Polish national anthem, while a violinist sits on a bench, happily performing Vivaldi. The mountains rumble a bit as if to say, "Don't forget us."

Life is back.

The villagers dress in their finest. Elders sit quietly to themselves, watching the younger ones dance and shout. Life is well again in the small village of Hoslava.

Soon, the traveling refugees join in the fun. They play games with apples, including the dunking game, and one in which small baskets of wooden toys are hidden around the orchards and the children skip to the beat of a drummer tapping out song typically played before war. Today, he plays it to celebrate the village becoming a small town, welcoming the refugees and the labor skills they bring. If they stay. Some are from other countries, also under the iron fist of Hitler; now they are trapped inside the Polish borders, unable to return to their native countries. They consider themselves subjects of Poland.

The festival runs through the night and nearly to dawn before dying down, a few bottles of consumed Russian vodka providing plenty of fuel. By midnight, the *dziadek* (grandfathers) of the village are half-lit with red cheeks and silly vodka smiles. Still feeling the rigors of the journey, Hober finds a place to make a small bed. He still prefers to sleep under the stars. No more church eaves, no more lucid dreams of God's messages. Tallal joins him under the stars, unrolling the prayer rug he has kept with him since Warsaw.

They sit near the fire Hober makes, not saying anything to each other, yet knowing what they are both thinking.

Hober feels a restless sensation, a new one. The mountains shift the ice during the night, cascading broken off pieces into the river, which carries the chunks to an offshoot tributary, creating an overflow. That will lead to flooding in the lowest points of the valley. Since the area is uninhabited, the excess water soon forms a new lake – one day to become a starting point for men to fish and restock their villages with food. It is the cycle of life on the tundra, a perpetual cycle.

Hober and Tallal awake feeling rested; the noise of the festival made no matter to them in their exhaustion. The journey took its toll, making the young men in the group feel much older than their ages. Tallal emerges very mature for a young boy, and Hober, now nineteen, feels as if life already slid past him in a rush, or drowned in the sorrow of loss. They become great companions, like brothers; the age difference does not matter to either.

In a short time, the other six refugees find homes with families who lost loved ones in the war. In addition, during the previous winter, a virus swept in and took some weaker villagers to the grave, leaving empty places in their homes as well. It is the wheel of life, recycling itself over and over.

Once again, the village grows, first slowly, then in metaphorical leaps and bounds. New homes are built before winter's harshness makes it nearly impossible. Friends help friends as long tables of harvest foods and breads are set for the workers building and reshaping the village, growing it into a small town. Hoslava, if she could speak, would say that life is fragile yet always prevails, and say it with conviction.

Father Miesko arrives from the church to take a head count of those needing confession after the festival. Those who yelled like the wolves at midnight when the dancing was in full force now deal with sore heads and aching throats. Red streamers sag from the damp air, the trees resembling red willows. While the oaks are aflame now, the upcoming month will sweep their leaves to the ground.

In the forest, animals also forage and stuff their findings into safe havens. Hober misses the forest, truly misses it. Soon, he will trek off into the woods to check the prisoner camp, making sure no one returned to restart such a place. But along with that is welcome relief: no longer are stray soldiers making their way through the village, nor is the train engineer sounding off words of war. Nor do threatening words come from the one wire that links Hoslava to the outside world.

All seems calm again in Europe. The entire continent begins to rebuild, as healing starts and families grow. Time is the greatest healer, though, as well as nature and her gentle hands.

Hober feels the future still holds much for him. He knows his destiny should reflect his upbringing. He wants to honor his family, the light of his soul, a soul he rebuilt himself on fortitude and endurance. He never wants to lose track of his friends and those he loves, but he longs for a different kind of love – not the pet love he and Angelica shared in their youth, but a true love that lasts a lifetime. He feels he has many qualities that will make him a great husband and father. Yes, he has plans.

But until then, it's nature and the mountains. While he sleeps, he dreams the other side of the Tatra calling him from the Ukraine. However, there is no passage safe for travelers, none found between the two peaks of the Carpathians, the mountains within the mountains.

The refugees settle into Hoslava as easily as if they have always lived there. Father Miesko found them permanent homes, just in time for the village to prepare for winter. The fields are bare, with remaining haystacks tied to the centers by heavy twine in the image of a fine lady's dress. The sun only sheds its sweet light for part of day, a sign of winter's approaching darkness.

Hober is growing quickly into the man his father would be deeply proud of, starting to live the life for which he would have hoped. There are only two things missing, love and family, but his father would say he was still too young to be married with a family. Yet, he feels the loneliness of no companionship. His young friend, Tallal, is already learning the Polish language, reading and writing from a very patient teacher; hopefully, he will master the violin, too, he thinks. Already, the village people have high hopes for Tallal.

Which doesn't solve Hober's dilemma. Love is an easy word to say, but a much harder thing to find in the village growing into a town. However, that growth does attract more females. He observes the incoming war refugees, and finds few men accompanying an overflow of women. They come because village life is safe and protective, a very good place for so many without husbands to begin new lives. Soon, Hober has his pick of girls to choose from. It is commonplace for village girls to marry young, since the men are expected to father many children to continue feeding Hoslava.

Another group arrives, looking worn out, mostly women dressed in simple country clothing. Their possessions are strapped to their backs, everything they own carefully wrapped inside bed linens. They look like they left with no choice given as to what to take. The sky opens wide and full of snow clouds; every so often a few flurries break away and drift to the ground. Soon, the village receives a dusting. Chimneys work overtime as their smoke lofts and fades into the coolness of an autumn that will soon pass.

Hober listens intently to the accents of the new people. They seem to be from southern Germany, Bavaria; there is a slight hint of French in their voices. The women's faces are more streamlined and their sweet creamy skin more noticeable than those in the village as they carry themselves with elegance, even when dirty.

Soon, he catches the eye of a girl, who glances back; they have a mutual attraction. Her skin is rosy from the winds, but her shoes, once posh, are now dirty and soiled. Still, he finds her a perfect woman who can still carry herself with pride, no matter her circumstance. He finds her even more attractive. Once, his sisters were of the same cloth as the young German. She walks with her family, glancing back at Hober. He looks to her as if to ask her name, too shy to ask directly. His imagination goes to work. "Pierrette, or Eva, or Helda... I wonder what her name is?" he says aloud, mesmerized by the new arrival.

The group of new arrivals finds themselves in the same position as Hober's refugees when they first arrived – no one has a place to bed down for the night. Once again, the church doors swing open and Father Miesko invites them in. They walk single file into the church, gazing up at the icons and rafters. The pews holding song books and the sweet scent of incense makes them feel safe.

Halfway through the day, food again becomes the immediate quest of the hungry arrivals. Now, the suddenly larger village has to maintain food rations to last through winter; more food items are pickled and stored away. Bedding and clothing also need to last, as very little washing is done when ice, frost and snow cover the homes. Clothes lines take on the appearance of frozen spider webs, and life again slows to a time for rest and rationing. The villagers give what they can to the new members. Never will there be walls or forbidden border lines; the village is always open, all for one and one for all!

As the new arrivals lie down, Hober walks into the church and sees the girl he has his eye on falling quickly to sleep. "Pia, why not stay awake with us?" one of the ladies says. "Let's all talk and come up with a plan to see if we will stay here or leave."

Pia... the lady reveals the beauty's name. "I'm too tired and prefer to just be left alone," Pia says. "I miss everyone, my father and brothers... please just leave me be."

The church grows quiet as their voices die down. The candles flicker, casting shadows on the overhanging gold dome, while the altar sits behind wooden shutters. Orthodoxy is a mysterious religion. As it turns out, the women are Huguenots from Northern France; they left for religious freedom, only to find the world upside down and themselves persecuted, barbed wire camps holding in religious people of all nationalities. After persecution followed them from France, Germany turned out to be a hotbed of more pointing fingers and judgements. These women came along way, in the company of just three men. The church feels comforting to the men, too.

Night falls on the emerging village town, Hoslava's seams spreading with new arrivals daily. Like its people, Hoslava has been through change. Beginning as a hamlet of pagans, now it was a Christian village holding Huguenots and Muslims, Jews and Baptists originating from all around Europe. Yes, Hober concludes, Hoslava deserves to be called a town.

Hober and Pia meet the next afternoon, a very windy day. She finds him huddled behind the ox shed, packing his knapsack. The coldness of winter shows itself in a heavy, weighty sky and drifting snow. His fingers begin to turn blue, yet he is diligent in his task of taking great care of his possessions, another of his father's lessons before he passed away. He looks up – and catches Pia's eye. The "love at first sight" has a chain reaction. He has heard many say what he now feels. And that is, Pia is one to know, and perhaps get to know in a permanent way.

She speaks softly, her Polish needing a little work as her French accent devours the rural local dialect. Her p's and r's roll gently, as in Polish, her words spoken quickly, a sound of heaviness to some who speak romantically in the native tongue. She finds him attractive, while he finds her as beautiful as the night sky.

"I cannot speak Polish well," she whispers.

Her eyes flutter; she finds him so good-looking, should he be speaking with her? He examines her face, lashes, lips and dark wavy hair as she does the same with him, noting his tall, thin body, shoulders that appear strong on a body that stands firmly but without the edge of an ego. She finds his voice calming as he speaks slowly, as though she were deaf.

"I can hear you, Hober; my ears are no longer cluttered with the shelling of bombs. My understanding of Polish isn't that bad. You don't have to speak so slowly, but I thank you for being so considerate."

They both laugh. Funny, how language, the great barrier, is also full of the sensuality of getting to know each other. As Pia continues talking, missing a few words here and there, Hober finds her more and more endearing. "Pia, if you'd like, I can teach you proper language," he says.

"I speak just fine, maybe out of turn or backwards, but I prefer to learn by my mistakes." She says it with wit. It's clear to Hober she is a live wire, the war taking nothing of value from her personality. He finds it a most charming characteristic.

The church bells interrupt their coy conversation, bits of flirting and moments of silence in between. Both are a bit shy. Hober wants to know more about her, but the time isn't right. The bells chime again, reminding villagers that mass awaits them.

The gold dome that holds the church bells is outlined by the pinks of an early winter evening sky. The townspeople flood inside, many faiths represented by their faces. In the church's beginning, very few non-Orthodox people would have entered. When Hitler began his siege, very few at all showed up, too afraid to pray. Many prayed inside their homes, some of which became checkpoints for Hitler's army. Luckily, the town only had a few slight mishaps with outsiders traveling back to their home countries. The church had always invited the wayward, but once that ugliness made its way into town, the church had to restrict who came in, and they needed specific reasons why they were in Hoslava.

The candles flicker as those who gather to give thanks look to each other in gratitude. If it weren't for the silent code of village live, Hoslava would not have a leg on which to stand. But the people truly took care of each other.

Finally, the hymns begin, followed by the chanters reading from the Great Book. Everyone feels the sense of humility and friendship. Tallal prays in his traditional Muslim way, on his knees and bowing to Allah many times, under the roof of the Orthodoxy. He and the others have come a long way; village tradition holds they will continue to do so.

The sounds of barking dogs blend with those of wood being chopped, the last remaining logs waiting to be turned into firewood. The small brook winding inside the town is dusted with snow. Everything has the "winter blue" feel and hue as Hober yawns and stretches his hands, wiggling his fingers in the air, refreshed after sleeping outdoors for what would be the last time in a long while. Smoke from the chimneys makes an intriguing design while hanging over the town. The clouds are dark and heavy as snow falls and drifts. Even the church bells chime in a muffled way, the snow wrapping itself around the iron bells. On better days, farmers would be heading to the fields; instead, several children sled down the small hill outside of town. Hoslava's one-track lane is filled with a mixture of snow, rain and ice, making it useless to walk, making traveling cumbersome. And working outdoors. Clean up after a war is lengthy, and the people get very little relief from the weather and war's other hard wages.

Hober still likes doing boyish things, even in hard times. He makes sideways footprints into the snow, shuffling his feet as he did when he was younger. Pia watches from her the window. "Hober, you look frozen! Come in!"

"That is a great idea, Pia. Thank you."

He enters the small home where Pia now lives with the family that took her in. They are waiting for him. "Pia, I graciously accept your hospitality," he says, trying his best to impress her.

He watches her move about the small cooking area, where a sad chicken stares at him from the cutting board, awaiting its timely demise when it becomes dinner. Everything about it reminds him of his family, yet he doesn't want Pia to think he is sad on this day… and most days. If it weren't for Tallal filling his heart with such need for protection, he would no doubt be depressed. He still recalls the death camp now and then, how it still survives in the forest. He doesn't understand the evil that lies in some hearts.

Pia hands Hober a warm cup of tea, the steam rising. He wants so badly to tell Pia he holds intentions for her, and wants to get to know her better. Her French accent tickles his curiosity, her eyes twin pools he has never swam in. War can make love so much richer, the aftermath of it recreating love as a driving force, rebuilding life.

After tea and the meal, the family invites Hober to sit by the fire. Polish people love to discuss things, sometimes kicking up necessary arguments merely to clear the air. He feels pressure from the questions they begin to ask; clearly, the family has adopted Pia as one of their own. "Hober, what will you do for work?" the mother, Carmina, asks with authority. "One day soon, living outdoors will grow tiresome."

"Well, Carmina, I have an idea on what I will do with my life… no worries," he replies sharply.

Hober doesn't care to sit any more. "Would you like some fresh air?" he asks Pia, thinking of taking her on a walk into the forest.

She is slightly put off by his question. It is already night.

Nothing but pitch dark, starlit skies would be their company. Is his invitation in good taste to walk alone with Hober, now that she has affection toward him?

She is unsure. "Yes," she suddenly answers a moment later.

The door closes on its own behind them as the winds kick up, the night feeling a bit wild. Hober realizes Pia is new to the terrain and isn't quite sure of entering the forest at night. Nor of the wildlife in it.

As they walk, Hober explains the positioning of the stars, that the North Star is used by trackers and mountain men. "Soldiers even use the same guidance when jumping from airplanes," he says. "None of this is by accident." He adds his upbringing and faith to the explanation that follows. His keen sense of nature and all things natural guide him, hopefully into a better life one day.

The stars illuminate the ground, bright as can be. Pia points ahead to the outline of the mountains, which appear even more forbidding. "How many men have died trying to cross those mountains?" she asks.

"People have only attempted to cross the mountains through the heart of the glaciers," Hober explains. "None were successful, as of yet. There is a shortcut from the foothills to the Ukraine, but no passage through the heart of the mountains."

As the two approach the forests, the treetops look as if they were Christmas streamers or a child's paper cut out. Pia finds it surreal. She has never seen wide open tundra, let alone walked in a forest during the night. As Hober reassures her there is nothing to be afraid of, a wolf sounds out. Pia holds tight to Hober's arm as he then tells her about the death camp he found, which left him with a fear that will never completely leave his sense of calm.

Pia quickly changes the subject. "Hober, why do the winds shift about so?" she asks, the world around her so different than the French towns, the only type of life she really knows.

"It is the winds of the North. They come here to collide and create the winters we endure."

"I once visited Paris," she says, then describes memories that reveal what she has seen in war. She recalls Paris often, she adds, to save her mind from the long road of horror she just experienced.

Hober listens, realizing he and Pia – and all the young refugees now in Hoslava – have seen things no person ever should.

Chapter Seven

They enter the forest slowly, Pia making sure she can touch Hober at all times. "Hober, what is it we will see?" she asks.

"Something large and monstrous, something I have not shown anyone other than you," he whispers. "The war has been here all the time. We just hid our heads under the church eaves, never taking notice of the sounds that came from the forest. I have discovered a Nazi-occupied camp this close to the village!"

Pia does not say another word. She follows Hober closely as he tramples down the wildflowers and grasses. She senses his reluctance. He drops his head as he walks further down the overgrown path.

In a clearing sit four bunkhouses, half-rotten from a hot summer followed by heavy snows. The timbered ceiling caves inward. Clothes are piled with shoes, wet leather scenting the air with decay. *When does this end, all of this sadness?* Pia wonders. She places her small hand into Hober's, feeling the calluses on his palms. A hard worker, she realizes, probably in the field and with timber. Her heart begins to race as they walk closer to the bunkhouses. There is no sign of life. Even the owl hides from the place, once his stalking ground for field mice. Nothing moves. No wind, nothing.

Pia sees the makeshift graves half-filled with stagnant

water, the dead buried deep. The most recent holes are small, for children, yet there is no sign of children nor any kids' clothing. No way a child could survive the vastness of the forest, she realizes, let alone the wicked ways of soldiers. But why are there no children in the graves?

She is terribly upset as a rain shower begins. Hober holds her. She gives him a slight smile as the raindrops glide gently down his nose and across his lips.

"Pia, I shouldn't have brought you here. I am not sure why I did," he says. She watches his lips move as he speaks. "You have seen enough war and skull and crossbones emblems of the death camps and the soldiers who marched the streets."

"I feel safe with you, Hober. Let's keep going," she says.

The bunkhouses take on a ghostly pallor. The slats of the falling walls spread further apart, creating a peek-a-boo effect that a child would try their best to find humor in, to occupy their minds. Now Hober begins wondering where the children went. He finds an old desk and reads through some of the official documents laying there – and finds names of children with numbers next to them, all in German. Now he has a strong idea of where they met their demise. With heavy, weighted snow covering everything in winter, children would be buried under such snow if left to fend for themselves. Perhaps the Nazis evacuated before anyone would find the camp they created off book, by their own doing, not an official concentration camp, not even in the records of war…

Soon, they walk back silently to the village.

The next day, Hober is set on finding information about the children. What village did they journey from? What country? Were they Polish? He did find Jewish belongings, but he has no good way of finding out; it was a secret camp.

Tallal approaches him. "What is it, my friend?" he asks in his rich Middle Eastern accent. "Your face looks as long as a winter night."

Hober gives him a shoulder shrug, not wanting to answer. "Tallal, my young friend, I have a secret that is a burden, and I am only one person who cannot change the world and war!"

Tallal is taken aback, though he knows something very disturbing bothers Hober and not to pry. Whenever he is ready, he will say. Tallal sits next to Hober, no words exchanged, just two young people contemplating the trials of life, their heads in the palms of their hands.

Hober learned something else in his reading of the papers in the camp: that the Germans stole most of the art in the countries they occupied, and most of the wealth. They hid the works in caves and old mine shafts, while raping whoever and whatever they wanted at any moment. From a few bypassing drifters, he has heard that the Germans took over more of Europe during the war than he realized. Not only was the war in surrounding countries, but Hitler devoured much of Europe itself!

Father Miesko posts a flyer to the church announcement board that *matins* will start up again, prayer hour for the villagers. God must be watching the horrors of man against man, the way He has allowed war to be made – time and again over the centuries, these are thoughts of those who have fallen under dictatorships. Time and again Poland has been invaded and left for dead, yet her people are truly salt of the earth, builders with an undying fortitude for life at any cost.

A mantra runs through Hober's veins, that one day he will truly make a difference, somehow. Perhaps he will never know the lives of the children from the camp, but he will pray for them. As church begins, gold rings holding lit candles and incense building up,

Hober finds comfort in the ensuing holy hour. He spends the time praying for the little children and all those lost to the war.

As she sits nearby, Pia knows she's in love. She feels a desire to marry Hober and deliver him sons and a life he can cherish and carry with him, along with the security that nothing can take she or the kids away from him. She also knows that wherever Hober goes, Tallal will as well.

Their bond is part of the family that has formed within the band of refugees, survivors of life and war, brought together from roads that led them to Hoslava, looking ahead to roads where they will go into the future. Images of life as light as a feather evolve into rebuilding bombed out homes and fields, while the bunkhouses, graves and avalanches create a place of delicate beauty and sorrow. It is sorrow that is the thread tying the villagers together. If one is hurt, it hurts all; the unity that grows from such tragedy, now giving more life to a village that has existed practically since the age of man.

Soon, Hober feels he and Pia need a change of pace. The village grows tired as people continue flooding in from the war for shelter, many with nothing, scratching what they can out of the soil. Then the stored potatoes become infested with an insect from a faraway place, turning the entire crop rancid.

He knows it is time to say farewell to the village and begin anew with Pia and his surrogate brother, Tallal. Perhaps they can travel to Hungary or even far north to Norway, where the skies are endless and food plentiful from the sea. Maybe they could stowaway on a ship to Great Britain, where many Poles had already fled, where Father Dominik now said mass. He has caught wind of the plight of what war left in its wake, the states of famine, the bombing of London, an underground filled with dirty-faced children and the elderly, teachers and mothers. Most of the men were still gone.

They sit beneath an apple tree on an unusually warm afternoon, eating a few crackers and one egg each, discussing their future life. Children or no children, they both have seen what man can do to each other. Did they want to bring children into such a cold, cold world?

Tallal is keener than ever to be part of this new family. He lost everyone in his own tribe, and embraces being family with a Pole and a Frenchwoman.

After a light lunch, they walk into the forest as the villagers prepare for a late harvest. They hold hands, his strong and hers delicate and small. They love spending time alone, even if only for a walk in the forest, something that has been part of his life since he was a small boy. The forest is damp, dew glittering from the pines, the small brook chattering away as always, talking to no one but itself. Chimney smoke scents the air.

Pia is a bit flushed; her cheeks are a light rosy pink. He finds her even more stunning and beautiful. "Pia, this is a big decision for us, on where to live. I have been here since I was born," he says. "My mother and father sacrificed much for us kids. Where will it be truly safe these days? Even with the war over?"

Pia smiles. "Hober, my place is wherever you are. I will go wherever you want." They walk a little further into the forest and discover piles of wood stacked like cones. The mist begins to weigh heavily. Fresh tire tracks line the mud, ploughed up from the wheels of heavy equipment. Hober is stunned. "Who or what comes to the forest again?"

He hears men setting up a camp in the forest but speaking in accents that resemble Brits. Perhaps this is a camp for the victims of war, a place for shelter and food, sustenance for those who truly care about the souls that survived.

Hober and Pia stand in the dark woods, watching the men build from the timber they have just cut. A large hole now sits in the forest, which makes him curious. "Why would the British choose this part of Poland for what looks like a Red Cross camp? Why not place it out in the open?"

Pia shrugs her shoulders, though she too is curious about the soldiers and the moves they are making. They listen intently to the men just as one slips up – and a German accent spills out. "These are not British aid workers," Hober whispers. "These are conniving Germans who will soon trick and fool innocent people into following them here!"

Pia senses Hober's alarm and cups her hand over his mouth. "Shhhh!"

He looks her in the eyes, and for the first time, sheds a tear. She grabs him by the hand and they make their way out of the forest.

After they are out of earshot, Hober asks, "Who do we tell? If anyone?"

"No one, Hober. No one! The last thing the village needs is more hysteria. Let's try our best to keep the village safe and calm."

Hober has a terrible feeling about this secret, but it is between the two of them, so he will keep it.

Meanwhile, the villagers prepare for the festival. After harvesting what they could after a planting season in which very little rain fell, they string bright-colored paper banners from building to building. This year's festival is low-key. The celebratory feelings aren't there, as in the past; the war has done what wars do, belittling the hard-working people of the tundra, who didn't even notice the avalanches anymore. They waited with baited breath about who the war killed. Father Miesko no longer rings the church bells. Mass is only held on sacred days, and no one enters the church unless called upon by the priest. He too feels the weight of the war and the sin that is the outcome of all this death.

The women begin their preparations for the winter months, pickling and smoking meats and fish. The tables are set for a small, festive meal together, and perhaps some dancing afterwards. The young women are dressed in bright colors, lace-trimmed dresses and silk-tied shoes. The men are dressed in the finest they have, dark trousers and jackets of heavy wool.

Hober never joins in the festivities anymore. His spirit is worn, and he has lost his joy for celebration, his interest in it. Pia understands his heart, heavy with worry for the villagers and the camps strategically placed in the forest. The tundra calls him no longer; the cries and growls of the great wolf and bear have grown silent. Much crueler beings lurk in the forest now.

Chapter Eight

Night falls unnoticed as the festival dwindles. Hober and Pia are very tired; *no more talking or discussing anything today,* Hober mutters to himself and not out loud. The French love to communicate, and he would never want to offend her. He kisses her goodnight and she hold his hand. "All will be fine," she says. "Don't worry so much." But he can't help himself. He knows what is out there in the forest.

The next dawn, men walk the small, main road into town in order as if soldiers, yet dressed in civilian clothing. Are they the men from the forest? Hober's heart speeds up when he realizes it is them!

He runs to the home where Pia is staying and calls for her to come outside. She meets him at the door. "What is all the fuss about?"

"Pia! Pia, come with me quickly!"

She shrugs her shoulders. "What is it, Hober?"

"Just run to me." His heart nearly beats out of his chest. "I will not lose another person ever!" he says aloud as the men walk closer, their pace quickened. "Pia, listen to me. Just run, just run, just run!"

Pia continues standing in the doorway, surprise by the alarming sound in Hober's voice.

It is too late. The men are well inside Hoslava. "This village is a threat... to whom? Goats?" one says loudly, his

German accent very clear. Hober recognizes him as the man from the forest; now he and the others have come as soldiers to take again.

"Pia, please run! They are soldiers, not aid workers. Run!" he yells again.

A soldier wearing skulls on his lapel makes his way to Pia and pulls her by her arm, forcing her out of the house. The soldiers shoot the women and children standing in the kitchen. Shocked, Pia freezes in place as Hober runs toward her, still yelling her name.

Suddenly, Hober feels a searing pain in his arm. He's been shot.

The villagers quickly barricade themselves inside their homes. This does not stop the soldiers. They beat down the doors and shoot most of them. Pia remains among the soldiers, and they begin to take her away, into the forest. Hober can't do anything about it; he's lying on the ground, wounded. So is Tallal, who has also been shot.

Father Miesko rushes from the church, running in his black Cassock to Hober and Tallal, both now semi-conscious. He carries the two indoors and tends to their wounds. They lie on the pews as incense from the Vespers still clings to the air. Hober awakens and whispers, "Did they take her, Father? Did they take her?"

"Yes, Hober."

He weeps as Tallal, also now awake, tries to comfort him. Father Miesko stands above them and begins to pray: "Please, please Theotokos, great one, please heal these two young men. I also pray for those who lost their lives today. May they sit at your right hand in peace for ages and ages…

Amen."

After three days of slipping in and out of consciousness, Hober awakens, alarmed. "I need to go to the forest to find Pia," he says.

"I will go with you and we will bring her back," says Tallal, his first words since the few he spoke after Father Miesko brought them into the church.

"I have to help her, Tallal. The soldiers just shot us and the villagers for recreation."

After Father Miesko gives them some food, Hober rolls to his side and stands up, a bit shaky and weak, yet more than ready. Adrenalin sweeps him out of the church, and also carries Tallal. He becomes Hober's wing man as they walk into the forest slowly, gathering their legs, then picking up the pace when their legs feel stronger.

The forest is oddly quiet. Each step they take echoes back to them. Uneasiness surrounds them as they make their way to the camp. "There is the camp," Tallal says softly. "There it is. Let's go get Pia."

The grasses are tall and deep. The echoes of mountain avalanches begin again, a sound very familiar to Hober. He recalls the sounds of the great owl and its signals to others of approaching threats. His listening skills are supreme and refined, due to years of living in the forest after his family died in the fire. He listens intently. No sounds from creatures… no men talking. As snow gently bleeds from the clouds, he senses something dire.

They sneak inside the camp – and find it deserted. Just like the last time, the clothing of those they took is piled on a cascading mound of cloth. No signs of anyone living. Hober looks at the death skulls etched on the doors of the wooden structures.

Pia is gone.

He falls to one knee, weeping into his palm. Tallal comforts Hober as best he can, yet how does one remove the pain of loss?

Pia is gone!

After Hober gets up, they rummage through the clothing and belongings from the Hoslava villagers that were taken. They also realize they are finding things from captives tied to another village, fifty kilometers away. Amongst a pile of shoes, Hober finds a familiar pair. *Pia's shoes.* The red string is still tied to her shoestring, something he'd done during the spring in jest, his way of flirting with the one girl he loves.

Now, she is nowhere to be found.

Hober spent years thinking his heart could never break again… but it does. Tallal keeps searching through the rubbish and finds Pia's handkerchief, still tidy and not stained from the rubbish pile. It was oddly pristine, as if just placed there.

Tallal decides to search the back side of the wooden building for more clues… and there she is. Pia. Lying on the ground. Murdered.

She lays face down in a half-washed away puddle, her arms tied behind her back.

Her hair is muddied, her underclothing halfway down her legs. *Oh God, she is gone.*

Tallal begins to pray for the words to tell Hober… and the courage. Finally, he finds Hober. "I found Pia," he says softly.

"Tallal! Thank you! Where is she? I want to see her, tell her how much I love her." As he says it, Hober senses in his heart she is no longer; he feels half of himself being taken away. How much he hopes his feelings are wrong...

Tallal guides him to the back of the building, where he lays his eyes on Pia. "No! No! No!" he screams as a flock of blackbirds scatter. "No, Pia, no! I need you to stay here with me!"

Hober is blinded by his anguish, his heart emptied by lost hope. Tallal quietly stands on the edge of the forest, keeping an eye out for his friend, allowing him to grieve. There are no winners in war. The words of the idiom are silently etched into all those touched by it. This time, men pretending to be aid workers did the killing, truly the evilest men of all.

Tallal stays awake with Hober during the night as Hober sits on an old rock near the brook. He says not one single word, shocked and dumbfounded by how the day began – and then what it took from him. At a distance, he can see the colorful festival banners still fluttering in the evening winds, the Tatra Mountains silent in the background. When night fully falls, it falls black.

The night is not kind. Hober sits chilled by his own sweat, tears stinging his face, his hands clenched in anger. Even though they say absolutely nothing to each other the entire night, Tallal is a deeply comforting force.

A week passes. Hober spends his time wandering the village aimlessly from dawn to dusk. Nothing much gets accomplished. Tallal tries several times to involve him with the new migrants continuing to settle into Hoslava, yet Hober wants nothing to do with them. The only thing he wishes to recollect is the day he met Pia on the road from Warsaw. His life feels over, even at his young age.

"Let us go back to the camp to bury Pia," Tallal suggests. "It has been too long to leave her laying in the wilderness without a proper burial."

Tallal is right. Orthodoxy tends to the living and the dead with full honors, usually in a prescribed time period after the death. He convinces Hober to return to the camp at midday, when the sun sits "halfway in and out of the clouds", as the villagers say. This casts a menacing hue on the wooden building, piles of clothing and shoe, dull colors outlined by wintry blue, suggesting a rendition painted by an abstract artist.

Pia's body lies right where Tallal discovered her, face down in the soil. The soil has since frozen, encasing her face in frost. They pry her away from the earth, as though fetching something out of a tiger's mouth. They tug and pull hard, as she was in "death's sleep." Hober pulls her undergarments back up to her waist, and the two carry her back to Hoslava. They arrive at the cemetery, dig for hours in the hardened soil, and finally place a makeshift cross over her after filling the hole. It marks her bed of permanence. She is with God now. Within a month, Hober speaks no more of Pia.

The village again fills with victims of the war, all displaced, all suffering. Hungarians and French journey to Hoslava after hearing of the villagers' compassion; soon, it bursts with people once more, the human waves entering the village staggering. More babies are born; more elders pass away. The church doors now remain open to those in need of prayer inside the golden dome containing Greek candelabras, a majestic golden ring sent from Greece as a gift many years before. It hangs over churchgoers that now come from multiple religions – Catholics, Lutherans, Orthodox

Christians and Jews all praying together as a village. Praying together in times of poverty and loss is the most important happening. It is not the "House of God" but the amount of prayer sent to Theotokos that matters most.

Hober never fully recovers from Pia's death. The images of her and the way she died, the way they took her, continually haunt him. She'd never been touched by any man, something she and Hober were keeping sacred for their wedded night. That would have been the moment of unity, her giving of her virginal self to him.

The next morning, a group of young women make their way into the village. A dark-haired brunette gives Hober a "look-see." She wears a mourning dove-colored dress, speckled brown and blue. Her hair is chocolate, and she looks to be twenty-something. Hober notices without truly looking, with Tallal observing Hober's eyes as they watch the new arrival. Tallal winks. Hober just shrugs his shoulders, as Pia often did. Who knows where love might land?

His days flit past like tiny sparrows; one moment turns itself into another and another, and then a season passes. Time and again, Hober wishes he could speak to Pia, write her a note of how deeply he feels for her... but once again, he is alone. He decides to write a letter of love, from the strong mind and gentle hand he always felt when in her presence:

My dearest Pia,

This war seems to be something that will never go away, something now a part of life as we in the village have seen our share of invaders. I had hoped to have the chance to share this life with you, all the goodness of a day and the sorrows that life brings now and then. Our children would have been gentle, kind and large-hearted, generous and intellectual. I miss you more than I can say. I miss my family and the things that would have been...

All my devotion rests in your palm from the heavenly place you now dwell in.

Your love,

Hober

After he finished, something came to him: A man comes to realize that life is no longer a game. No more tossing of marbles into the dirt to click away the weaker marble. Life is full of struggle and joy.

Chapter Nine

Tallal feels lonely as he watches new faces make their way into the village every day, its borders now bursting, the village now a town. Migrants with little to call their own pitch small tents and later cut timber from the forest to create new homes, slanted roofs and small gated gardens lit brightly with small tundra flowers, lily of the valley and white daisies.

The women who arrived days before are settled in. Hober has made up his mind that love hurts too much after seeing the broken but still beautiful women focused on their survival. He is fully disgusted with the pain love leaves behind. He looks away, and in his look Tallal senses his sadness. "Come on, Hober, it doesn't hurt to look at the art walking themselves into the village. These people are created for the eye. We humans are works of art... take a look!"

"I'm not interested, Tallal. Leave it alone." Hober grunts out the words.

Tallal turns away and sits on the drystone fence, counting the women, calling aloud the colors of their hair, as if giving them nicknames: "Brunette with wide smile. Blonde with blue eyes! Redhead, strong-willed." On and on he goes.

The church bells chime twelve. The men working the potato fields come in for a light meal, then back they go. Storage of potatoes is vital for all seasons, as villagers still worry about running into the same parasite that created the famine that struck hard in Ireland, even though it's been almost a century. Word travels of the plight of relatives that escaped the Nazis, only to find themselves in other countries also dealing with hard times.

Hober feels like his life is idling, moving in very slow motion. What to be? Where to be? How to empty the memories of family and the camps of war? What to do with the piles of clothing and bowls of gold fillings from the teeth of those exterminated by the S.S.?

He feels he has aged tremendously. His youthful look fades into that of a man with a tired soul, longing for love and a place of security and tranquility. Yet his love for Poland is so strong, from the steam engines that arrive from Warsaw and their thick coal scent lingering among the low, heavy tundra clouds to the village to the people. How could he ever leave? Because of Russia too many times forcing a regime on the gentle Poles, too many invaders from centuries past, the Nordics taking away any hope for a wealthy Poland, he well knows in his heart that one day he may need to leave.

The church only draws a few loyal followers. Religion is not the order of the day, but he hopes it will soon return. The church has become an eclectic house of worship; while Orthodoxy built the church, the wayward without countries now pray inside the gold dome.

The Feast of St. George arrives, making it a day where Father Miesko presides. The villagers fast for a day, and then the feast and celebration bring ropey breads and honey, salmon cakes and pear halves, pickled beets and the precious egg, colored in bright reds, blues and yellows. Because of light rain falling on the cloud-filled day, the celebration is held in the small church hall, crammed tightly. Tallal worships in his traditional way, praying to the East. Once again, life fills with simple pleasures, if even for a day.

A bolt of lightning crackles above Hoslava, striking a tree and splitting it into two. The runaway trunk shatters, spreading small pieces of wood everywhere. Villagers hide their heads in fear, especially the migrants, who know all too well the sound of missiles. However, this is a lightning bolt, a nature-sent missile. Hober walks outside to see the stricken tree, the very same tree in which he sat as a boy, a curious owl listening to the village women speak of community life. They never knew Hober was absorbing it all like a human sponge, some gossip, some God's truth.

Now the tree was gone, another part of his youth going up in flames. Hober is beside himself. No one can help, not Father Miesko, nor Tallal...

How many times has any of us thought about the future? For some, it is a daily routine, as it is for Hober. The future is as bright as one makes it, with the aid of the great creator – Theotokos. But now he is distraught, looking into a future that feels without love.

More people file into Hoslava. Hober scans the younger women, who are now accompanied by their grandmothers most often, so many men lost to the fields of war. They come from all ethnicities, worn and eager for a fresh start as word travels from one location to another that the war is a thing of the past. The men rest eternally in bunkers and forests, never to be buried in the town's cemetery, but forever immortalized in festivals of remembrance such as the Festival of the Dead.

A day of hard labor awaits the men. A recent storm has dropped a number of ancient oaks that then need to be cut into firewood. The men's stomachs lead them to the forest to take charge of the downed trees and haul them back into town. They distribute the resulting firewood evenly and fairly. Though it's green, it will burn with enough hot kindling to ignite it. Later, the stoves are ready for baking apple dumplings and sugar cookies with the little precious sugar remaining; it is in short supply. The hands of women wearing aprons are coated in flour.

Hober joins the men in the forest while keeping the dark secret of the prison camp to himself. He does his best at guiding the men through the tundra, praying to God the fallen trees are nowhere near the camp. He promised himself long ago he would not give up its location, to not create mass hysteria for people already leading lives of uncertainty. As he and the men approach the fallen trees, a hawk cries while flying in the cloudy sky. Hober glances upward to the hawk, knowing it is on the hunt. Survival of the fittest… yet the prisoners had no chance to defend themselves against the Nazis. He doesn't care about the beauty of the sky.

After such a devastating loss, only Polish determination gets him through… thank God for that. He knows he will survive and try to live a life so profound that maybe one day, the forest of edgy honesty and poignant beauty will be the guiding hand that replaces his missing family. Maybe love will blossom again like a spring revival.

His original migrant friends, those he led back from Warsaw, have been moving on. Vladislav made his way back to Macedonia and married his love, Maria. Mariam became a correspondent after the war, reporting on the migrating souls, now homeless. She moved to Paris, where her small flat has several bright pink cherry blossom trees and a tiny park across the street. She clacks away at her typewriter, bought by her father on a long-ago German holiday. *Her writing is backed by pure honesty; no better person to tell the world of the travesties of this war,* Hober thinks.

Tallal also longs to move from Hoslava. "Hober, let's leave, let's just go!" he says in a slightly begging voice.

"To where, my friend? To where?" Hober asks in a doubtful tone, but one tinged with hope.

"The world is not only in Poland. Where I come from, life is the sea and the mountains and the snow of spring and the dates that fall from trees. My home is rugged, and she is beautiful. We could go there!" Tallal misses his home terribly.

"Tallal, I'm not going to claim I know much about your home," Hober says. "I do know ancient history, and your land has been as filled with turmoil as this land. If we are going to set off and leave Hoslava, it will be to a somewhat peaceful place, if at all possible.

They walk slowly from the forest and rest in a small clearing in the tundra, their knees up against their chests, Hober's face in his palms. His signature link. Time is now of some essence, he thinks. He knows his heart will always be heavy for Pia, but life moves on. It's time.

As the seasons change again, Hober no longer gauges life by the harvest. Now it is by time itself, the starkness of time. How to find that one special person to share life with? While Tallal is a great companion, he is not the answer to the love dilemma… though he knows the boy will always be in his life, one way or another.

Chapter Ten

The day of decision arrives, the day of plunging into tomorrow and the future. The flow of refugees into Hoslava dwindles, and the parade of women trickles down to a few distraught, wayward souls. Some soldiers, much kinder than the Germans, again turn up lost, unsure which direction to take to their homes. Some have no desire to ever return, and others choose to live nomadically, now that war has taken away a secure roof; the roofs of bombed-out buildings can topple inwards and crush both bone and spirit. Nomads are free in a sense, Hober thinks, more so than a person who lives under a roof in a village once targeted by the enemy and occasionally bombed by accident. Human error in war is happenstance.

Tallal can feel the shift in the air. "Hober is ready to soon say farewell to this town that once was a village," he says quietly. "He is ready to say farewell to the church and the memories, the goodbyes to the forest and tundra, the shifting of the Tatra snow peaks, the thunder of the avalanches. Better days are now the hope in his mind."

There is an order to farewells. The timing needs to be perfect, even though Hoslava will go nowhere and will always be welcome for Hober to return, if need be. The festivals and celebrations and harvests will forever run in his veins.

Hober already knows the elder women will be the hardest people to bid farewell to. Since the death of his family, they have looked after him as much as he would allow, strong in will, the best cooks he would ever encounter. They know how a man thinks with this stomach as well as his heart. Hober feels he can easily stand on his own two feet, with Tallal as his self-appointed sidekick. Their war memories go with them always, like worn leather shoes, but they have lives remaining, and are ready to walk their way into a new future.

Soon enough, they find themselves high above, in the Carpathian Mountains, walking a treacherous passageway very few have traveled. The ice is frozen solid, rock formations jut out from the hillsides, and the timberline switches from whistling pines to stark nothingness as they climb higher. There is no greenery of any sort.

Hober slides his knapsack onto his left shoulder, opens it and eats an apple, purposely dropping the seeds in the half-frozen soil, curious if they will take root by some miracle. He has no idea yet on where to plant his own roots. He does know the village holds too many memories. While not all bad, some memories are fierce and strong, and he now desires peace in his quest for future love and family.

The cutting edges of the frozen winds brush against their faces, turning their cheeks a purple-red and snow binding Hober. Neither were prepared for weather this fierce or land this stark. While Hober's love of the mystery of these mountains never left him doubting their power, he still is merely a lowlands farmer. The wickedness of nature in the Carpathians is more than he ever imagined.

As they climb, Hober and Tallal soon find it difficult to

breathe as the thin air takes hold. Their mouths gasp open and shut, mimicking a fish out of water. Hober's lips are dusted in frost as life shifts into something dangerous. They are facing a place that only a handful of skilled mountaineers have been – or even attempted. The Ukraine beckons in the winds, on the other side. Hober's thoughts of a better life to be gained by crossing the mountain range seem impossible as his hands freeze, and the winds continue to blow relentlessly.

Night falls over the frosted land. They do not possess coats or mittens thick enough, nor scarves; their clothing is threadbare and of poor quality. They are not well prepared for such an endeavor. As the night becomes a black curtain, they huddle against each other while sharing stories of Tallal's early life in Pakistan, and how a visit with relatives trapped him in war-torn Poland. Hober's voice quivers as he tells of his family. This gift of storytelling draws them even closer, sharing experiences both had so prematurely in their lives, more than must adults ever endured in pre-war life.

It nears midnight. The creatures do not make a sound; nor do predatory birds. A perpetual coldness, stagnant white coldness, grips the land. They eventually fall asleep as the snow stops at their feet, the frost curling in the shadows of snowflakes fused to the ground. "This is a treacherous place, yet the beauty if more than I could ever imagine," Hober whispers, his mouth made bone dry and stripped of any moisture by the altitude.

"Hober, perhaps this is too much for us," Tallal says, his voice crackling from a dry throat. "Let's leave and turn back in the morning."

"No, Tallal, please… let's give this a try. Okay? I love you, my friend, and I will not place you in any further danger.

We will turn back tomorrow if it is the same as today, but if not, let us go on." Hober speaks with a quiet, confident authority.

They fall back asleep, huddled together, shivering against each other, Hober a bigger man than most his age, and Tallal a man among children.

When daybreak arrives, Hober sighs. Hard-driving snow blinds the two as the sun seems to be sitting on top of the place they slept. The altitude remains breathtaking, literally, leading Hober to his decision.

"Tallal, this has always been a dream of mine, to come to the place of the avalanche and blue glaciers, yet we are merely village farmers. It is best to return to the village. Do you agree?"

"Yes, Hober, I do. This place is too powerful."

They descend the snowy slopes, happily greeting the timberline, then the song of the brook. They hear songbirds as a great elk glides past them, his antlers as majestic as his stride. The familiar sights offer great relief. Hober feels at home.

Hober can't help feeling let down after arriving safely in Hoslava. He wants nothing more than to leave the town and its memories, yet the mountains are too fierce. He will try again to cross into the Ukraine and will find a faster route. He will not give up.

The village is oddly quiet. Chimneys are missing their constant trails of lofted smoke. No farmers are in the fields; there is no one in the town center. When they walk past the church, it is boarded up with plank board. All is too still. They slow their pace as they approach the first home on the main road. No one runs out to greet them with eggs and breads.

Now, Tallal is alarmed. "Hober, something is wrong. Where is everyone?"

He looks around. "It seems someone came while we were in the mountains and took the town and everyone in it. The priest… everyone!"

"Who and why? Why would anyone come to take a town? Time are now changing into a peaceful future… I don't understand."

Hober rubs his hand across his cheek. They are exhausted, chilled by glaciers and carrying empty stomachs. But now, there are no grandmothers to wrap them in wool blankets and feed them warm milky soup from a proper bowl.

Something terrible happened while they were gone.

"Hober, come over here!" Tallal exclaims. "There are tracks in the mud, tank tracks and heavy tires, as if many trucks have come and gone."

Hober runs over to take a look. It is true: people who have not understood that the war was declared over continue to come and take away. Pia's death is nearly more than he can withstand; now all the people are missing!

"How do we find them all, Hober? We have to search for them… now!" Tallal had grown to love each resident and the priest; they became his adopted family. Now life in Hoslava seems to have ended in several days – in the blink of an eye, their world was gone.

They pack what they can into their knapsacks and begin to follow the heavy truck tracks, loaded down with human cargo. They run into a band of teens that made their way into the forest to hide; together, they continue the search. The young band consists of six boys and four girls, all frightened and angry.

"What happened? Tell me," Hober asks.

"The Germans came in and told us to form groups by age, which we did. We were frightened to death," one of the girls replies. "The soldiers' guns were pointed at our heads, so we did what they said."

"I don't understand. Why would the soldiers take the entire village… and how did you escape?" Hober still can't believe everyone has just – vanished.

"We ran away while they were burning numbers into everyone's skin like cattle. We can quickly into the forest, and we waited there for them to collect everyone, watching helplessly. We knew if they caught us, too, that would be the end of all of us."

She speaks quickly to Hober, as if her words are capable of choking her with the disgust all of them feel. The Germans, Hober knows, leave no one with any defense. They choose older people first and then use up the resources of youth, targeting the younger people to do their labor while elders are cast into furnaces. In cleaning out the village, they wipe away ethnicity. Gone are the ones who hold the village together, the storytellers, healers and anchors of village life. His heart suddenly aches for the elders, along with a need to protect the survivors, as he did on the road leading out of once Bohemian Warsaw. He grows more and more angry as the pain transforms him into a soldier. He and Tallal are turning into renegades, freedom fighters alone the ten young townspeople.

The group of young freedom fighters gather things they need from the vacant homes, writing notes explaining what they took:

Dear Mija,

We borrowed a loaf of bread, four eggs and milk, a few biscuits and a couple of candles and lamp oil. Oh! And of course, a few blankets. We thank you from our hearts and we will find you and bring you back, and in this we will also set this right on the things we have taken from your home. A szczere dziekuje (a heartfelt thank you).

Sincerely,
The Woolly Fighters

They decided to give themselves a nickname. This band of young, tough foot soldiers wrap themselves tightly in the grandmothers' wool blankets, their only means of protection since the Germans stole everything of value. Now they search for the contents, beginning with the people.

The world feels larger again to Hober. The group looks to him as the leader, since he is well-organized, has a keen sense of nature, which paths to take, which grooves in the road mean more when it comes to finding the villagers, even the way the wind blows leave upside down, warning of an incoming storm. He feels again in charge of human life, but his heart strings pull hard knowing that Father Miesko was even taken, too. If it weren't for Father Miesko, and Father Dominik before him, Hober would have dived into the deepest end of grief.

As they set out, Tallal marks a few words into the cold, damp soil with the end of a pointed stick:

Here we come, one and all – we are the Woolly Fighters and we will *restore the people to this ancient village once more. That is a promise that* will *be kept.*

"We are one!" they cry out together, their voices

mingling between the shifting pitches of puberty and the deeper, more settled tone of young adults. A small falcon flies above them, eventually landing on a tall oak as if to say, "I will be here waiting; go get the people back."

The second day dawns early, even though the band didn't make camp until late into the night. Some stagger stiffly from the hard bedrolls, while a few yawn and rub their eyes as Hober takes a head count. He is not about to let anything happen to the group, fully understanding his responsibilities more than ever before. There is no time any more for him to have the light, airy laughter and memories to care him joyfully through life, which is what most youths have. He understood early on how fragile and serious life can be.

After the head count, they all crouch near the small fire, eating from tins and breaking bread. Forgetting their Orthodox morning prayers, they devour the food and begin walking further down the road, following the large heavy grooves in the mud... tire tracks, German tracks, the wheel marks of thieves who steal humans and kill farm animals out of hatred... but hatred for *what?* The soldiers of this lost German patrol are evil, with no regard for any life. Not only do their demented minds cause them to search for Jewish survivors to take prisoner; they also take what they can and kill for the fun of it!

The sun never finishes rising on the grey, dull, dimly lit day. The Woolly Fighters walk on. Hober watches from behind, observing the small frames of the young people, all thin shouldered, with thin legs and arms and woolen caps resting on the boys' heads as the girls wrap bits of material around theirs, creating makeshift babushkas. Hober feels even more protective as he recalls the head protection the grandmothers gave him after his family died. He, again, promises himself he will not stop until he finds the townspeople.

The Woolly Fighters march inside the grooves of the tire marks while singing an ancient song the elders taught them. It is a song of pride and fortitude and love of God, exactly what keeps them deeply motivated. The Germans are notorious for picking on what appears to them to be weak people. The elders are not weak at all. They are just tired from another long winter of starvation and survival.

"Let's take a rest," Hober says.

The band sits and eats one egg each to keep strength. As Hober opens his knapsack, he notices clothing hanging from a branch on the edge of the forest. He recognizes the material pattern – the colors of the ancient symbol of Hoslava, red and blue and thinly striped. He runs to the material.

There, lying piled atop each other, are the elders of Hoslava… all dead.

The Germans killed them because they were too slow and took up room inside the trucks, room the lazier soldiers wanted. After making some other elders walk the distance, they promptly killed the grandmothers.

Hober throws his hand over his mouth. "Oh my God!" he screams into his palm. He lifts his hand. "Oh my God!"

"What is it?" Tallal asks, approaching, already sensing what lies behind Hober's cry. When Tallal arrives, he begins to cry, drawing the attention of the others. They gather around and stare at the piled-up bodies of the grandmothers, all dressed in their cloth of village colors, now dead and gone.

They arrived just a bit too late.

Later, after nightfall, Hober wakes from his bedroll, screaming. "No! No! No!" Tallal wraps his arms around his friend, and they begin to cry together. The others remain asleep, fulfilling Hober's wish, as they will need to sustain their stamina. He has a feeling the road will be long until they find the survivors from Hoslava.

Hober sits on the ground, holding his chin to his palm. *What a life this has been so far,* he thinks. *Where does it end? When I move to the land of freedom? And where exactly is this land of freedom?* He has traveled to Warsaw, the Carpathian Mountains, the Tatras and her echoing avalanches. Where he can he go now to heal himself and his kindest of friends, Tallal?

Day three arrives. The band gets closer to the German convoy. The heavy trucks leave an easy trail for the group to follow. Soon, the furthest up front, Tallal, is close enough to see familiar faces gazing back at them through the flaps of canvassed trucks.

He slides away, then races back to Hober. "They have not killed them all," he whispers. "They are in the backs of those trucks. How can we get them out of there?

"We will wait and wait until the opportunity allows us," Hober replies. "I don't really want to kill a German soldier... but if I have to, I will."

The response surprises Tallal. Hober's command was to never take life, but the circumstances have changed that. Now he is angry and wants back what is left of the villagers. That, too, was a promise.

Truck exhaust blankets the low, damp soil with a grey cloak, which has created the opportunity to see who is alive in the trucks. They see few sets of eyes looking back at them. Not yet known to them, the Germans have killed so many, more than half the townspeople, either burying them along the way or tossing them from the trucks to be reclaimed by the forest.

Hober has had enough. There's a line of no return, when one is heartbroken over and over again. His anger feeds his power, turning him into a man of experience and pain emerging from the dirty faces of the Woolly Fighters. It's all about ensuring survival now, survival and a future for whoever remains.

As the day nears its end, Hober sneaks up and spies on the German camp. The trucks form a circle around a large campfire, the accents of the soldiers echoing from the forest haze to the Woolly Fighters. Hober knows enough German to translate: they are planning to move the remaining people to a camp near Rutka, a town on the border of Poland and Belarus. They will leave the prisoners as "gifts" to the Soviets, to do with them what they want; the men are from the Soviet army, also refusing to acknowledge the war is over. The Germans are growing tired of the remaining people, according to the words Hober hears, and will be relieved to rid themselves of the cargo. Hober's anger grows further, tempered by a strategic question: who remains? How can they get to them?

He returns to the Woolly Fighters, who wear nothing more for armor than the village grandmothers' hand-stitched blankets. How will they rescue the surviving villagers?

Then the answer hits Hober: during his time alone in the tundra, he learned to make himself seem invisible. When the wolf or bear sniffed him out, because as the animal itself.

That is what he will do to counteract the Germans.

As night turns from twilight to darkness, then fills into deep blackness, the fire's embers drop to a low glow. *Our chance,* Hober realizes, the Germans passed out on the ground or in the trucks after drinking vodka most of the night. He silently directs the Woolly Fighters to take military weaponry, attack, rescue the survivors and get them back to Hoslava.

As the hour strikes three on a German soldier's watch, he awakens to find all of the guns swiped. When he looks up, Hober and the Woolly Fighters open fire. A few soldiers run into the forest, where they will become lost or eaten by the wolf, karma never too far away.

After their stunning victory, Hober insists on burying the dead soldiers who fought the band. Tallal wants nothing to do with any burial ritual for the bastards who killed innocent townspeople, his new family. Hober finally agrees, and the lay the soldiers in a pile of death to decay into the forest floor. Noticing the massive mound of flesh below, a falcon calls out to its kin for a feast in the late-night hours among the animals of the forest.

Dust to dust.

By the fifth day, the weary townspeople Woolly Fighters walk through the night and into the next day, moving quickly to return to Hoslava. When they arrive, Hober thinks of the loss, not just the villagers, but also German mothers who were waiting for the return of their sons. That will never take place, due to their wickedness and defiance of peace time.

Exhausted from leading the rescue mission, Hober and Tallal make camp under the open sky. They say little, wondering if they will ever leave Poland. If it weren't for

Tallal, Hober thinks, the pangs of being alone would devour him alive.

Soon, the welcome sounds of church bells and voices fill the town. The band of Woolly Fighters separates, their job done, and the teens settle once more into Hoslava. They get on their knees and pray for the safe return of those who fled into the forest to escape the Germans but have not yet returned. Hober feels claustrophobic. Hoslava is home, yes, but home with too many sorrowful memories. He wants life to be about love and contentment, a future, perhaps a profession, a wife and a few children... somewhere else.

As they sit, a country's name keeps running through Hober... *America.* The word is, America is safe. This rings through villages throughout the area, and Hober tells Tallal he is thinking about it.

"Hober, I cannot go to America," Tallal says, insecurity in his voice.

"My dearest friend, wherever I go, and you go, my home is always your home," Hober responds. "I cannot stay here. It is no longer home for me. My buried family is a daily reminder that life changes quickly. My childhood friends are all gone, and Father Dominik and Father Miesko have filled my heart with the knowledge of Theotokos power. I respect that more than I do any man and will take this as a lesson to find a happier life.

"I really want you to come with me, but I understand. You must do what is best for yourself." His own words hurt, but Hober loves Tallal so much that he knows he must offer to let him go to find himself.

"Hober, dammit! I am not going to leave you. We are friends and that is that," Tallal replies firmly.

"Okay, then that is that. We need to sort out which direction to head. To the sea? Or to the mountains once more? Or South? Where?" As he finishes speaking, Hober finds himself frustrated by his own impatience.

The next day dawns in bright yellow streamers strewn across the blue blanket sky. Hober feels a change coming his way. His heart races with anticipation, the thoughts many as he is still trying to decide where he and Tallal will venture to.

Within moments, the skies fill with heavy gray planes. His heart seizes; *it can't be...* He quickly breathes a sigh of relief when he realizes they are American supply planes, bringing food and blankets for those liberated from the camps and bombed out villages. Celebrations continue to break out across Europe as more people realize the war is finally over. People in Britain dance in the streets. The French toast the liberating soldiers as they walk through the city, toasting the brave men who freed them from Hitler's evil, five-year hold on their country.

Hober and Tallal follow the planes, watching where they start to drop their landing gear. Tallal chuckles and Hober smiles broadly as they watch a plane land with ease, which amazes them. They have never seen such a thing. They'd only known the train that came to Hoslava station every other week, sometimes once a month. Yet, this massive mechanical bird can easily land on the nearby tundra, a natural strip of barren land, the words painted in red on its fuselage so welcoming: "Red Cross". When it touches down, they hear a thud that reminds them of pieces of timber hitting each other as they travel down the river to the mill.

They run to the plane, not considering the danger of the powerfully spinning propellers, wide-eyed and eager to see who emerges from the small silver door. They look at each other joyously, flashing wide, carefree smiles they haven't worn on their faces in a very long time. It brings both back to the realization they are still young, Tallal much younger than Hober, and not yet old men as they sometimes feel. They imagine what the belly of such a plane holds – maybe men coming to aid the hungry and tired, and to establish once more the security of the village, the power of their human spirit rising again.

They stand patiently, waiting for the door to open. When it does, a small troupe of Red Cross aides walk down the shallow stairs, nurses and other women there to hand out food and blankets, fresh water and bars of soap. The villagers lack warm water for bathing, but right now, the brook and river will do. Some run from Hoslava to the plane, to be greeted by the friendly faces of aid workers. Many fold their hands in prayer, thankful that the war has ended, while sorrowful for all those lost and left homeless, some without a country. Now that the village is alive again, the flow of migrants coming in on the one main road resumes.

The aid workers shake off the long flight and begin their duties straight away. They hand out bread and dish warm soup into tin bowls, and wrap the townspeople in warm, clean wool blankets. This so moves the people that they huddle closely together and begin to pray, something most have not done in a very long time.

Hober and Tallal approach the tall, dark-haired pilot, who is opening a can of beans. Hober thinks quickly of the English his mother taught him, summoning it from his deepest memories. "Hello, I not speak English too well. Where you come from, if I can ask?"

The pilot holds the can of beans in one hand, his leather gloves in the other. "What the hell is up in that sky?" he asks. "You people live literally at the altitude of the moon! I nearly plummeted several times on descent. Those strong winds must drive you crazy, I know it would me!" he gruffly spouts.

Hober recognizes the man's accent. An American. "Where do you come from?" he asks again.

"Chicago, USA." The pilot speaks each word loudly, as if Hober is unable to hear or understand.

"You come very long way," Hober says.

The pilot is taken aback by his comment. He assumed Hober wouldn't know where either Chicago or the United States were. Fortunately, Hober's mother was gifted in the study of world geography and educated him the best she could before the fire.

After studying Hober and Tattal for a minute, the pilot grins. "Well, I see you two have been through a lot, probably more than most kids that lived through this ugly war. What do you need from me, kid? If I can help, I will." The pilot sounds like he's yelling at them, but they realize it's because the propellers are loud, like the plane cabin, like the war.

Hober looks to Tallal with the eyes of a child opening a Christmas package. The miracle of flight has descended upon Hoslava in more ways than one.

"We want to go to Holland, to Amsterdam. Take us there?" Hober asks bluntly.

"What for, kid? There is nothing left there. I mean n-o-t-h-i-n-g!" *Did the kid realize he was asking to be taken to another bombed out country?* the pilot wonders.

"We need to find ship to America from Amsterdam," Hober continues, unfazed. "In Amsterdam I collect few refugees to take with Tallal and me. So many my age, no parents... I want to help them if I can."

"I can't take you and your pal there," the pilot responds. "First of all, as I said, there is nothing left of Holland, not one thing that you both need to go get involved in. Secondly, I have rules to follow; the plane isn't public transport. It is commissioned from the U.S. government and I do what they tell me... got it?" He is losing patience with the young duo.

"Poland is lost and not restructure for very long time. If ever," Hober says.

"I agree, son, Poland is a great country. I have some Polish roots and connections to this country as well. My father, mother and I immigrated to America when I was a small boy. I too could have ended up in the same position as the both of you."

Hober stands his ground. "Then you know what freedom taste like... no idea what that would feel like," he says. "America, they say, um, sweet like butter. Skies change in different places people. Work plenty, people are kind." He shares the news he once heard from a migrant.

"Well, you have a point as far as I know about what freedom tastes like. Kid, though, I have to tell you that some immigrants aren't always welcomed with a smile, if you know what I am trying to say."

"I understand," Hober nods. "We too see, um, prejudice in Poland. What is your name?"

"Myscha, but you can call me Mike, since you aim to live in America," the pilot replies. "Get used to not using your birth name."

Hober smiles. "Mike, your Polish name when I was child, my grandmother gave it to mouse eating our bread and cheese." Tallal begins to laugh; being young men starts to feel wonderful to them again.

The pilot looks at Hober and returns his smile. "Hey kid, you are a little bit of a smart ass, but I like that. That's why you have survived, is my guess."

The day drifts into the darkness of the tundra. Mike sleeps inside the cabin of his plane as the remaining townspeople build a giant community fire, hoping to draw more hidden neighbors out of the forest and into their homes. No one emerges. They realize the people in Hoslava now are all that is left of the town… now no more populated than a hamlet. Very few are left alive by the Germans or saved by the liberating soldiers.

By midnight, all the aid workers find places to bend down for the night. They set up tents for themselves or for refugees continuing to walk the lone road. The fields lay unattended, the corn already plucked and eaten by birds. They, too, are hungry and in need of a safe place to call home. But the forest has also changed: the bear and wolf no longer sound out at night. The death camp stole the spirit of the woods and its creatures. Nothing is the same.

Chapter Eleven

There is a nameless star that Hober tries his best to find each night, insignificant to most. He first set his eyes on the star the night his family died from an innocent harvest festival celebration that turned into a raging fire. The star's light, its anchored place in the sky, becomes Hober's good luck piece.

Once, a Sunday school mate gave him a rabbit's foot for good luck. In that soft, bodiless foot, Hober realized we are all prey to something or someone, and he would never take another's life again, like he did while rescuing and retrieving villagers. His bullets that took life, and the men they took, still lay on the edge of the forest. So much death and decay, all of it underneath a universe holding much more power than any soldier or any man.

During the night, Hober decides that it is finally time for he and Tallal to leave Hoslava and the mountains for Holland. He sees The Netherlands as the edge of the world, its ships that set sail from its harbors for destinations across the world, traveling beneath the foot of Great Britain, the ships skimming her majestic lands. He begins to envision the sights the two may see on their voyage to America. Little do they know what they will see in Amsterdam, victim like most of Europe to the Great Atlantic Wall, built by Hitler's men. It reached as far as France, keeping the targeted in and the saviors out.

After the night passes quickly, dawn makes its statement, brightening the sky and pushing the darkness into its place of rest. Hober feels free in spirit as he awakens, knowing Tallal and he are about to embark on an adventure that will lead to a safe place to call home, a safe place to settle.

Meanwhile, Mike begins to refuel the plane with the first of several old barrels of fuel that rolled off a Nazi convoy truck. The villagers scooped them up and hid them away, and Hober knew where they were stored. He and Tallal roll them out and Mike quickly funnels the liquid into the plane's gut. After sputtering for a few moments, the engines ease into a reliable hum as the aid workers begin to board. Along with two villagers, now part of the crew.

This time, Hober and Tallal do not say any goodbyes to villagers in Hoslava. They walk on board, sit down and buckle up. Within minutes, the plane takes off, the gears clattering from the wheel wells as the landing gear rises and climbs inside. The sensation of taking off tickles the two. They laugh all the way to thirty thousand feet as Mike reads off the altitude and speed gauges to his eager passengers with his lovely American accent.

The smell of oil blends with the perfume worn by female aid workers. In it, they sense the air and the roads and the sea that will lead them to America. Tallal tells himself he can return to Pakistan one day to visit any remaining family members, or to Poland to visit relatives who fled Pakistan for freedom – only to land in ugly chaos.

As he prays to the east, Tallal thinks of how the two will both be *The Boy from the East* once they reach America, sharing life under the liberating arms of the Statue of Liberty.

A few hours later, the plane lands on a partly bombed-out strip in the outskirts of Amsterdam. Hober and Tallal exit, knowing they may never see Mike, the American pilot, again. They give him sweeping hugs and shake his hand. Then, they stand at a distance as the plane takes off from the cluttered airstrip, the bomb holes and their blackened explosion markings making it rough for Mike to hold the plane on a straight line as it gains speed. Soon, the heavy gray bird flies off into a sky holding the pale tones of sea shades.

What a contrast, Hober thinks, between the blue harbor and sky lit in feathery colors.

    As the plane disappears into the clouds, they take a look around them. Amsterdam is still smoldering, the beauty of its buildings obscured by pock marks and blackened craters from bombs that hit their marks. It looks like so many other places in Europe, but they are only in Amsterdam for one reason: to find a ship steaming to America.

    After an hour, they are still looking at the entrance of the clouds, into which their new American friend flew his gray bird. They have no idea which way to walk to reach the shipyard. Tall, glorious windmills turn slowly, a few still turning despite broken blades that clink against the wooden structures. A chill runs up Hober's spine. This empty place once held vibrant life. Like Poland. The bright colors of the windmills remind him of the cloth his grandmother sat for hours darning into dresses and tablecloths for the family.

    Haze begins to roll in from the sea, dropping low over the canals. Hober and Tallal walk into the city on a long, narrow road. To their right is a small canal used to water the tulip fields. The canal holds bodies of several people that had been executed after being taken from the city. Their bodies lie halfway in the water, bloated and disfigured. They do their best to ignore the sights as they walk over stone and iron bridges, down small alleyways and along more canals. Houseboats gently rock back and forth from the tides leaking in. The city feels quiet and angry at the same time; not only did the invaders come, but they transformed Amsterdam into a second Berlin. City streets remain cluttered with belongings, furniture and more bodies. They hear echoes of voices but cannot see where they are coming from. The haze from the harbor cloaks the city and creates a wall for the voices to hide behind.

They begin to fear the worse: more vengeful German soldiers paying no mind to the fact their regime has surrendered? If so, then when will the war truly end? Even though the peace and surrender treaties were signed, some men are evil and forever hide behind the act of war. Some of Hitler's bunkers still burrow into manmade hills, while they see parts of the Great Atlantic Wall that cemented the inhabitants of Amsterdam into a small area, the same effect as the Warsaw ghetto.

It leaves Hober and Tallal mentally and physically worn. Instead of filling with the joy of youth, as young hearts should, theirs now carry the knowledge of men.

Finally, the voices fade into the haze. They walk into the Zuidoost District and find a kind man more than eager to escort them to the shipyard. An older man, their guide sees in them two pairs of eyes much older than their bodies. He recognizes help is what they need. The man thinks of his young boy, which the Germans took to fight as a Nazi, forcing him to attack the very people he loved. On the second day of the Amsterdam invasion, he was shot.

The man guides the two to a small alleyway, his wool coat full of moth-eaten holes, his brown eyes tired and weary from war and grief. He sketches out a map for the pair to find their way, reach the shipyard and sail off to America, in case the trio are separated.

Their ensuing walk feels like it takes hours, the sounds of distant explosions and crumbling brick not comforting them at all. Sounds of people talking on the other side of the haze, and the sight of a few people cleaning up, are enough to unnerve anyone, Hober thinks.

Finally, they make their way into the shipyard. Tall ships bob among the hulls of passenger ships, leaving Hober and Tattal startled. They have never seen such majestic ships. The plane was enough for their minds to absorb; now they are trying to make sense of the ships' monstrous appearances. Their guide wishes them well – then turns without another word and returns to the smoldering city.

"Goodbye, dear sir, thank you so very much," Hober wanted to say. But he had disappeared into the smoky haze before Hober got the chance.

The ships and their gangplanks roll out for the passengers, but not one single person is waiting to board. Then Tattal realizes something. "We have no money to pay for a passage, Hober! What are we going to do?"

"We can wait to see if anyone shows for passage and borrow some money from someone… or we can stow away in the lower decks."

Within minutes, Hober figures out his plan. They *must* make passage to America. No turning back now.

"Okay, Hober, I am with you, you know that," Tallal says.

There is no other as devoted as Tallal, Hober thinks. His family is nearly gone know, and the remaining relatives will always know his dedication and love for them.

The two stand for hours, waiting for others to arrive. Night descends as they decide to wait it out some more. They unroll their bedrolls and sleep near the ship's hull, beneath the shadow made by the moonlight. The ship sways gently in the rise and fall of the tide.

Hober falls asleep with his eyes closed, but his ears awake, worrying that the Germans will march straight to them and take them as prisoners. He can feel paranoia rushing in from the general lack of sleep and shelter.

He feels more desperate than ever to find peace for them in a peaceful land.

White and playful in the night sky, the stars take Hober back to Hoslava and life before the war after he awakens, restless. He recalls the festivals of harvest, the church celebrations and baptisms, the scent of wildflowers in the tundra in autumn, the sounds of the great avalanches. He rarely sheds tears over memories, but now he sobs, holding it inward as much as possible so Tallal never knows how truly frightened and heartbroken he is. But Tallal is awake, too, listening to Hober's suffering. This has to work somehow, he knows, and somehow, the free people of America will happily welcome them into their country.

Daylight breaks the night sky open, and the rising sun awakens them. They quickly get up in anticipation. If the ship leaves without them, they will have to wait a month for the next departure... that will not do it for Hober. Now he wants desperately to be in America, to place his memories far back in the recesses of his mind, and to begin a new heritage in a new land, hoping to find love and have his children live near him while an older man. Ages before, Tallal made up his mind that Hober's dreams were his as well. Soon, they would share the dream of living in America.

They roll up their bedrolls and put them in their knapsacks. As they tie the last safe knots for their belongings, a man approaches them. "I must inform you the ship's departure has been canceled, by the orders of the Reich," he says. Even though the war is over, the Nazi presence continues to be strongly felt.

Disappointed, Hober wraps his arms around Tallal's shoulders, knowing the two now need to find food and better shelter. "My friend, we have been through enough and it seems we just can't get an easy time of it," he says. "Let's go find a place to bed for a few days and search for some food.

"Okay, my friend. I go where you go."

By noon, the sun casts its yellow-orange glow on what Dutch architecture remains. Blue doors are adorned in Delft tiles, while below them, the canals are filled with German amphibious boats. A few dead, bloated bodies float past. Tallal and Hober look the other way; they've seen too many dead bodies. They sharpen their focus on shelter and food as they begin to await another departure to America. Every second feels like an eternity.

Across the street, a Dutch woman watches them walk along the edge of the canal.

"Hey! What are you looking for? Your mothers?" she yells.

Hober doesn't find her invasive question humorous at all. He tries to ignore her. But Tallal, now angry, fires back. "No, lady, we are looking for your momma to tell her that you are nothing but a mere nuisance, and I also think you are very, very rude!"

Hober nudges Tallal's elbow. "Come on, is that all you have to say to her?"

"I think you want me to get into a tiff with this meaningless woman!"

"No, Tallal, not me. I wouldn't want anyone to end up hurt."

Though tired and edgy, Hober smiles while taunting Tallal. Time to lighten up the day, he decides, poking some fun and happily ignoring the rude woman and other women of the streets. He and Tallal have much larger ambitions, to find shelter and food. That is the plan.

Then he spots a menu board outside a small café. The menu looks wonderful, and while neither has the money to spend on extravagances like meat and cheese, an egg or two will suit them well.

Tallal and Hober walk inside the dimly lit room and see a man at a bar drinking hot coffee, stirring the cup in a daze. This man has also seen his share of war and death; his face says it all without words. They order two eggs and bread apiece, and for an additional wonderful treat, two cups of warm Dutch cocoa. While placing the cups to their lips, they let out contented sighs. *What a wonderful day this has become,* Hober thinks.

After their meal, they make their way through an alley. Clothing and wicker baskets lie on the cobblestone street, unattended. "This looks like it's free," Hober declares. "Let's take whatever we need. No doubt the original owner is dead, and the items will just sit here and mold under the seasons.

"Take what we need. No worries, Tallal, God will

understand," he says, certain of his words.

After picking out clothes, they roll them up and stuff them into their knapsacks.

Hober smiles. "See, Tallal, Holland has been good to us." His smile is so contagious that Tallal returns it.

They remain in Holland for the next week, finding temporary shelter. The café owner lets them use the sub-floor of the building. It's damp yet feels good to have a place to return at day's end. The ship to America seems cemented into place; the Germans are still not allowing anything to leave the harbor. Hober feels confident, though, that they will soon be aboard the ship – eagerly.

Exploration is the plan of the day. They walk past museums and chocolatiers as the Germans reclaim the gunnery and vehicles they brought to Amsterdam; many are simply leaving and heading back home to Germany. The rusted steel that remains in the city streets oddly resembles the skeletons of those Hober found in the forest. Shops remain empty and the tulip vendors gone; glass greenhouses sit empty. The city was colorful and alive before, and the future mends all things. Hober wishes for Amsterdam to again be her fullest self.

Time seems to take more than it is giving. The two grow impatient, waiting for word the ship can depart. Time feels stagnant as a pond of ash and sorrow.

Hober thinks back to when his life was fertile with friends. Now, he sees Tallal as his only friend, the boy's unexpected dedication to him worth more than he could ever truly say. Life would have been much more difficult without Tallal and his friendship. Once they land in America, Hober hopes he will meet other Poles and Slavs and form a community from which they can prosper. The word across Europe is that the great steel mills of Northeastern America need able hands and bodies. European factories are nearly vacant, as so many civilians entered the war and never returned to their homes and families. Soon, immigrants will replace those who came before.

Hober grows more and more keen on life in America, no matter the negatives or struggles he will face once he arrives. Will a family he does not yet have be waiting for him there, in the land of golden streets and silver roads? He is proud and his willpower strong.

The liveliness of the city seems unusual. Voices carry across the canals and people emerge from sub-floors and attics. Soon, Hober and Tallal realize why the Germans are making their final departure! The cheers and rallies take them by surprise, yet they too shout out what everyone on the streets is shouting: "Liberation is ours!"

The sky fills with celebratory fireworks, and the elders make their way to the streets to share whisky and bread. They wear their finest, which is now worn and threadbare, but appreciating what they do have. Meanwhile, the Germans pull out to shift their attentions to going home and cleaning up their defeated country.

Hober turns to Tallal. "I think we might do better if we try our luck at the harbor now," he says. They run back to the sub-floor space beneath the café and grab their knapsacks and bedrolls.

When they arrive at the harbor, they see people speckled across the deck, mimicking busy ants on an ant hill. The whistle blows several times as passengers walk the gangplank. Hober and Tallal quickly walk on board; the ticket taker refuses to take their fare of passage. "Country kids!" he barks out. "You have to purchase a ticket before boarding."

They turn away, disappointed, knowing they do not have enough money for the passage fare. Then, Hober schemes up a plan, putting away the Orthodox voice in his head. Certain things must be done in times like these, things he would never do unless he had to. Hober's mind explodes with desperate planning. He watches the porter leave the gate to the luggage and storage area at the bottom of the ship. It is now open – and inviting.

They sneak inside and hide behind large crates of cheese and whisky headed to America. They do not care the least if the month-long journey across the Atlantic Ocean is harsh and uncomfortable. They will do whatever it takes to leave Europe and give the future another chance to begin in a new land.

Soon, the ship sways gently. As the tides lower, the ship and portholes are at ground level as Hober watches the porter return. The door is wide open, the luggage room filling with wonderful sea salt air, the scent of adventure.

Once at sea, the ship cuts through monstrous wakes, making the two uneasy at first. They have never been inside such a majestic vessel as a ship; the lakes near Hoslava are shallow and clear enough to see the bottom. On the sea, the bottom cannot be found, only the indigo blue water and whitecaps, the splashing of ocean against hull and bow. The engineering electrifies Hober, but Tallal feels that if man were meant to cut across the ocean, God would have given them fins! He will remain nervous until the shores of America are in sight. Then he will calm himself.

After their first night onboard, they grow more comfortable with the sounds of the rudders and giant blades spinning to get the ship across the waters. They are invisible to the other passengers, no one knowing they are stowaways. This is the break they've needed for a long time. Nothing seems as if it can stop them from their plans now. They are soon to become citizens of America!

It doesn't matter that they have very little for a new beginning. Their knapsacks are stained with blood from when they buried Pia and the elders, their shoes worn after bringing them this far, the inner wounds of their souls and the people… one would think their dreams were impossible. But they have a future purpose, yet unknown, not to be known until it takes place.

Weeks pass and they remain unnoticed, "borrowing" food from the kitchen when the cooks complete their shifts. They listen intently to the language the cooks are speaking, English, but they get the feeling this might be "seamen slang." Still, it is always good to know what things to say to reply to the Ellis Island customs officers, where so many other Slavs and immigrants passed before them when entering America. Hober adds to the bits of English he was able to communicate to Mike, the pilot.

They make it through the whole month undiscovered, with no incidents or alarms, the voyage nearly complete. They are eager to emerge from the ship's belly and onto land, anticipating the air to smell of hard work and unity. The ship has been a very good temporary home, a new memory set in their lives… exactly the fuel to keep them motivated.

The whistles sound as the enormous ship arrives in New York Harbor and begins to dock at Ellis Island. New York spreads out ahead like a gleaming jewel, the Tatra Mountains now nearly on the other side of the world. Hoslava lies deep in Hober's heart, never to be diluted. His devotion to Poland remains forever, as does the spirit of his family. There are no longer ghosts following him, but a family that devoted their love to him, nurturing a future man of America, a man bound for greatness.

The railing slips into place with a loud scrape and halt. They've made it.

They jump from the open door of the storage area to the wooden docks of Ellis Island. Hober and Tallal checks their pockets for their papers, rummaging through each pocket to pull out wrinkled sheets. Hober's notes that he is a twenty-year-old Polish citizen of Hoslava village, in the province of Wielkopolskie; Tallal's reads that he is from the village of Abalapur in the province of Kalat, Pakistan, he a very young man. Tallal, himself, is not sure of his age, and his original birth certificate was burned in a fire when his village was bombed.

There is much chaos as people shout to the men tying the ship to the dock. Passengers fight their way to the gangplank. For some, the ship did not seem up to standard, since it was also used as a makeshift hospital during the siege of Amsterdam. Yet, it did its duty and transported them safely to a new country and a new beginning. What more could anyone ask? Hober and Tallal embrace each other, and silently thank again Mike, the pilot, who flew them out of Poland and into the ruins of the once beautiful country of Holland.

"Europe will rebuild," Hober says softly.

But for them, the new life is *right here*. America. The air does smell of freedom, its familiar sea salt blending into the haze of the grand city of New York. With the cool air refreshing their skin and the long journey now behind them, the first issue at hand is to smile at the immigration officers and then find work, pray hard, and pray for work with good pay. They have no idea how many others have already landed with the same idea. The Italians had fled during the Diaspora, and now once more were fleeing the aftermath of war, along with most of Europe. *Work is an easy word to say,* Hober thought. *Yet maybe harder to find.*

Chapter Twelve

Hober and Tallal find out that Sag Harbor, out on a place on the other side of the city called Long Island, is looking for Polish immigrants wanting to farm. They had their hearts set on mill work, rolling steel and working near the enormous slab furnaces. But beggars can't be choosy, they know; after being humbled into a nearly submissive life by the war and overcoming much, the window of a new life is all they see. Hober is not quite sure if he and Tallal belong in the city, the greater priority being to go where the work is. But farm life is what they left behind in Poland, and Sag Harbor will have to do without them.

New York City is alive and reckless. They make their way through the streets, buzzing with the hum of taxis and Navy sailors still returning home; the servicemen are also looking for work. Jobs are given first to them, if they find work worth taking. Wages dropped after the war, and life for many seemed like starting over again, reuniting with families and wives. The work for women really dried up, not nearly as plentiful as during wartime.

Now everyone seems to be in the same boat, and Hober knows he and Tallal are very inexperienced in the American way of life. They learn quickly about the pecking order and realize they will struggle once more. Every day, they stand in queues, waiting to be chosen for work in one of the steel mills.

"There is no work for you, boys," the foreman says. "Go home, or better yet, go back home to wherever you came from. Leave the work here for our boys returning from the war."

They keep hearing "No work!" or "We are only hiring returning servicemen!" Then one day, Hober overhears a man speaking about a place called upstate New York, and a city called Buffalo. He and Tallal chuckle. It brings to their minds the Wild West, the stories they secretly listened to on the ship through the ventilation system, an early education on the vastness of the United States, the stories consisting of tall tales blending with fact.

They refocus on the business at hand and decide to head north to Buffalo for work in the great sheeted metal mills, steel rolling out of them like honey. Time and again, though, they learn the hard way to take things said to them with a grain of salt. This wasn't one of those times. They knew they had to leave New York City and go to where the work was, but now knew they wanted to live in the city once they grew used and accustomed to the liveliness. Anywhere else seemed dull, terribly dull. But New York wasn't going anywhere. The pair would one day return to the congested streets, Hober knew, to where the neighborhoods edging the city filled with immigrants, one group bleeding into the next.

They begin their journey north with a free ride, hopping the second to last car of a nearly empty train. A few men sit in the rear of the boxcar, not saying a word, eyeballing Hober and Tallal. They have a story, too, yet the two pay them no mind. They know tough men when they see them. After seeing Nazi stares and empty hearts firsthand, it is obvious that certain men are just void inside. They stay clear.

The train glides, and then sways and clacks over a road crossing. The slats in the cars are spaced wide enough that they can see straight through to the passing trees and landscape. The thought leaks into Hober's mind of similar boxcars carrying human cargo to extermination in Europe. He closes his eyes... Pia and his family... the village... his dreams.

He seems to sleep yet is wide awake in his memories, not easily forgotten. The train rolls along, rocking all the people on board into a state of shelter and hope.

After night flashes by as fast as the landscape, they arrive in a train station with a large iron sign in black: "BUFFALO". Dark smoky clouds fill the sky. The train station holds solicitors for bed and a meal, places for working men to rest their heads. Men walk past the two, their faces dirty, their speech muffled by coughs, the coughs of steel mill workers. It will be hard work, Hober and Tallal know. The conditions are poor, but they are more than eager to begin and to save enough money to return to New York, buy good homes and find good women.

Hober begins to feel his Polish roots fading into the red, white and blue of the American flag. He wants to find other Poles to reunite with his heritage. He knows no one can wash away their beginnings, the blood trail leading back to their ancestors, their roots. He hears other men speaking with Slovakian accents, a few Polish, a few others Hungarian, and some Ukrainians. Tallal feels out of place, though. There are no mosques in Buffalo, no Muslims, no one that resembles him in any way. Hober is his best friend, yet he knows Hober is not his kind. His prayers are not the same, and he worries life may feel lonesome. But he has hope for the future: he also knows New York City *does* have mosques and women and the Muslim life.

Their first order at hand: finding shelter. This time, they find one room with one bed. They take turns sleeping on the bed and floor. The outhouse is used by all the boarders, and the kitchen is centrally located in the old boarding house. The cooks are hearty Irish women who cook equally hearty, great meals. As Hober and Tallal eat, they realize how much they have missed meals like this. In the morning, they will begin their new jobs as rollers, rolling the steel, a very dangerous occupation. Hober's sense of humor begins to return, with Tallal the recipient of his pranks. He nails Tallal's lunchbox to the bench in their room. When Tallal tries to grab the pail and walk away, he bounces back on the bench. Hober laughs out loud, a good, healthy laugh.

When the bells ring, the men rush into their jumpsuits, pick out their lunch boxes that the kitchen staff filled, and walk into the gray mill building. Smoke rises from the brick stacks. So begins a man's hard day for good wages, the first day on the job for Hober and Tallal.

Fortunately, their foreman is from Warsaw. He tells them he has lived in Buffalo for nearly five years; he and Hober then launch into a good conversation about politics and work, speaking in Polish. Tallal begins his duties straightaway and remains silent, knowing he is judged by the Catholic steelworkers. It seems religion should be most welcomed in a place like this, where men can and do die from the liquid steel pouring from blast furnaces, slipping beneath the heavy presses. Had they had a chance to have last rites given them, they would have felt more at ease in their deaths... in the mills, Tallal concludes, any religion should be welcomed.

The Irish immigrants pour into the mill as quickly as the Italians and Eastern Europeans, steel work being one of the most sought-after jobs. Work is a gift for these men. Hober works in the station next to Tallal, always keeping a vigilant eye on his adopted brother.

Weeks turn into months. The seasons change, one after another, until Christmas is once again upon them. This year, Hober realizes, it will be one of celebration. He will introduce the tradition of breaking the Oplatki to Tallal, a tradition part of Central Europe for centuries, the breaking of the wafer to begin the Christmas vigil. Hober wishes to make the holiday memorable for both of them after walking away from the bloodshed in the forest, how it stained the snow with human souls. He wants to honor the saving grace of those who led them away to safety, the people who helped them, like pilot, Mike, the old man with a good heart in Amsterdam, the city people who guided them to shelter and food, the goodness of people, the war now finally behind them. This fragility of life keeps him humble and thankful.

Snow storms blow over the great Lake Erie and into Buffalo. It blankets the gray mills and ices the river and brooks. Hober reflects on the time he explored the foothills and Tatra Mountains, the endless rumble of avalanches, pines tipped in white as the animals grew silent. He loves the snow and the "healing" feeling it evokes. He begins to feel like he can think back to memories of Hoslava, of life in Poland, without the severe stabbing pains of loss. Time does heal. It doesn't remove memory, yet it heals.

During Christmas season, Buffalo sees more snow than they have in ten years. Storm after storm falls relentlessly on the city. The mills close; it is too cold for the men. Hober and Tallal are left with a few others who have nowhere else to go for Christmas. The boarding house workers have left, which leaves Hober as the cook. On Christmas Eve, Hober makes sausages and eggs, a loaf of bread and warm milk, beet soup with vinegar, and a few slices of cheese. The simple meal suits him and Tallal just fine, and they celebrate with a few strangers. Life has brought them together as adopted brothers of sorts, and shown them the unending will of man to forge ahead. Christmas will always mean more than just another day in another year.

The city is eerily quiet, the snow soundproofing the noise created by passing cars. With the café closed, the small band of men remain in the boarding house, telling stories of their pasts, their families, how far they traveled to find work. Some have been in America for twenty years or more; they are the patriarchs of the boarding house. "Once you have saved what you need, you should return to New York for a better life," one of them says, giving his advice. "Buffalo has its down side, and the mills one day may not produce such quantities of steel any longer."

Hober takes in his advice. They save money and save it well. Since they live in a boarding house, they have very little to spend it on, so it is easy to save.

Christmas Day itself arrives. Hober and Tallal sleep in a bit as the other men fix tea and eggs. The scent of toast climbs the stairs, making its way into their room, Tallal resting on the bed and Hober on the floor with a heavy duvet over his head. "My friend," Hober says, "when spring arrives, we must leave."

"Okay, my dear Hober, I am bored with Buffalo anyhow.

We have enough money to start over in New York. I am ready and able." Tallal's voice skips in his excitement.

Finally, it's time to go off to New York City again. Buffalo has served her purpose; they found work and made it enough to return. Funny, how life circles itself now and then, in this case two young immigrants making a giant U-turn. They return to the city the same way they arrived, by open rail car, men sitting in the rear smoking and laughing. They join in the laughs, their time in America heading for the better.

Chapter Thirteen

The train spits them out at a depot where steel exports usually depart. They smile at the thought of being exported. They made it; they are in America to live as Americans in the land of hope and freedom.

After paying the fare for a bus to Brooklyn, they run into Miss Margaret, who is from the Yorkshire Moors in England. She was a caretaker of orphaned children during the London bombings. Her eyes and heart fill with compassion as she helps the two find affordable housing on a rent-to-own basis, which is something new.

This leaves Hober and Tallal happy, truly happy, and now happy without hesitation. They have the opportunity to own their very own homes, with their gardens and mailboxes hanging near their front doors, places to rest their minds and spirits. *Their* places. God has been kind to them, and to the fact that Miss Margaret takes a fancy to them straightaway.

She cooks and bakes for them, spoiling them with her meals and her protection. She assumes the role of an adopted mother; a boy or man can never be too old to welcome a motherly figure, a matriarch. She even chooses their small, quaint homes, and pulls a few strings; being immigrants, loans for home do not grow on trees for them. But she makes it happen. This is where their lives will unfold.

When they move in, the homes need a little fixing in.

First, though, is finding steady work. Hober applies to a nearby shipyard, while Tallal makes new Muslim friends who own a nearby café. He wants to own an eatery one day, and the work and friendship at the café is most welcome. He feels as if he now belongs to the city of New York.

A week later, Hober has finished painting his new home a pale yellow, also planting tulips in the front garden and thinking of what he will do with a small vegetable garden plot that lays fallow behind the house. He and Tallal sit and reminisce about the war and their old friends, his in Poland, Tallal's in Pakistan and Hoslava.

The season continues its change as people sit on park benches and the air fills with exhaust from cars and, on occasion, salt from the city's brackish rivers. New York is bright and gleaming. By contrast, in Europe, grieving mothers carry the weight of the world on their shoulders while their nations need to be rebuilt. The continent needs to be repopulated, and death needs to forever remain in the graves. Babies and families are desperately needed. Hober thinks of this, and also how disease has spread among the villages as the decay of human and animal corpses bleeds into the air. As a result, farms and shipyards are at a standstill. The Nazis did most of what they came to do – to end Europe as the world knew it and create a non-existent Aryan race. Even though he took his own life, Hitler's shadow still is present.

Tallal sticks his head out from his bedroom window next door. "Hober, take down your laundry. It's raining!"

He leaves the windows open to allow the cleansing breeze to sweep through, a very European thing. Their homes are almost atop each other, built to conserve heat in the winter. They allow very little room for cold air to skirt between houses. Hober is thrilled with Tallal being such a close neighbor, hopefully for a lifetime. The bond between them is unexplainable. *Perhaps death may draw us even closer*, Hober thinks, *but we've already been through enough at our young ages to last several people a lifetime! Friends we are, and friends we will always be.*

Work goes well for both, providing a simple life. There are no grand balls at the Ritz, nor strolls through Central Park. Brooklyn holds their hearts. Their neighborhood is filled with all sorts of ethnicities. The summer evenings become electric with the sounds of dialects and languages, neighbors sharing food and air time as radios blare out the evening news. Hober cleans his best pair of shoes nightly and sits them near the front door; the shoes he wore from Poland to America still have their soles and can carry him anywhere. When they eventually wear too thin, he will store them under his bed and pull them out now and again to recall his youth. He will keep them for the rest of his life.

The rain soaks Hober's clothes. He smiles at Tallal's worries. "What is a little rain going to do to me, after all?" he asks. Tallal is a sensitive boy, and what he endured has scarred him deeply and made him worrisome, when he was once a carefree boy. The war took much, so much.

After they settle into their new jobs and homes, Hober gets word from relatives in Poland that they too are leaving Europe for a better life in America. They want to stand on their own feet again, and live the pay it forward way of life they once knew in Hoslava. Hober decides he will give sanctuary as the church does. The village life, surrounded in unity, leaves no one out in the open. Life is to be shared, and the people fleeing Poland to come safely to the United States is a gift that pleases Hober deeply. His family will grow and expand in America, and love will blossom.

He has also met someone new, Sylvia, whose family already adores him. Now he has a large American family, as there is always room for more at the table. Celebrations of food and tradition temporarily wipe clean the slate of war and death. With that, Hober finds love… and love finds him. Tallal also finds the place he belongs, with his friends at the café. And, he too finds new love.

Life changes in subtle yet profound ways, and Hober's life is becoming a tapestry of woven threads: the orphaned kids and teenagers he aided from the camps on the lost road, the people he saved from the Nazis. Not one time has he thought his actions extraordinary; he did what his father taught him to do.

A dance is on tap at the community center. Hober and Tallal attend after inviting Sylvia and Magna. The girls arrive separately, but soon make very good friends with each other. Big band music echoes into the streets, and sweet laughter rises from the community center. Miss Margaret has arranged the event for young people to meet and get to know each other, and it is a success. As she placed orphans with the right families, she succeeds in matching Hober with Sylvia. Tallal's friends did the same to put he and Magna together. Life becomes again as it should be, a mixture of hard work and simple pleasures, music and laughter reverberating in the room and in their hearts, the boys holding honor in their hearts for their own struggle to arrive in America.

Life is good.

Spring breezes arrive to dry the clothing on the lines. Residents tune radios to their favorite stations, and the windows open all day once more. Hober and Sylvia grow in their relationship and move towards marriage. Tallal takes it a step faster, marrying Magma, who then has their first child. They immediately tell Hober he is the uncle. He is proud to call them family, as he is Tallal's brother.

Hober and Sylvia's wedding is celebrated with a small gathering of friends. The service is held in the garden of the church. An outdoor wedding is all Hober hoped for on this special day. Sylvia's wedding dress is a hand-me-down from her sister, a beautiful dress with tiny ivory beads that dangle from the bottom like spring raindrops. They exchange wedded rings, simple gold bands with their names etched inside of each. Tallal serves as best man, a very proud best man. Afterwards, there is a small reception at the community center, with another fifty people arriving to celebrate the bond of Hober and Sylvia. The priest blesses them for a happy life filled with goodness, which Hober takes as a very good sign. Life itself is a blessing, after all.

During the reception, the community center fills with music once more. A Polish meal of pickled beet salad, bread and eggs. Perogis and kielbasas. The eggs are a symbol of good luck, though Hober had his fill of eggs in Europe, wondering when such good luck would begin.

Then he looks at his new wife, and Tallal. It has definitely arrived, making life comfortable and him content. He got his cousins settled after they arrived a month before, then he bumped into a second cousin who informed him that he and more family had been in the country for years and already become American citizens.

As summer arrives, Hober puts his weeks of envisioning a garden to work, planting a beautiful garden in the backyard plot. The sun seems to be in full bloom as well. The rivers fill with tugboats, while on the streets, taxis skirt back and forth with passengers. Tallal has saved enough money already to purchase his own eatery, and Magna is pregnant with their second child to accompany their daughter. They pray this time for a boy. Tallal realizes he could use some help in the eatery, and truly wants an heir to whom he can pass the restaurant.

Meanwhile, Hober works at the shipyard and helps his cousins who left the city to live in Sag Harbor. He learns to love his journeys to the Sag. Cousin Maria greets him every time with homemade apple dumplings and warm cream, something Sylvia has not yet mastered. Her mind is more set on giving Hober a child, but she's beginning to feel all hope is lost. "All in God's timing," Hober calmly reminds her. Sylvia curses at his statement from her ever-so-positive husband under her breath, yet she prays her heart out for a child. Hober's mind is dead set on work and his newly found family.

Then, he learns Tallal needs some repairs to his home. "Hober, you spread yourself too thin," Sylvia says sternly.

"Why, I have time to spread around, and you know I love you the most," he says, squeezing her inside his arms.

"Hober, I wish you would be serious now and then."

"I have been that grown, mature guys since way before most men have to! Please let me be," he replies, softly nudging her away.

One week later, the news arrives that Hober has been waiting to hear: "Hober! Hober! I am pregnant!" Sylvia exclaims, running to him as he opens the front door after work.

He lifts her into his arms. "Sylvia, I am so proud of us!"

After spending a few minutes with her, he runs to Tallal's home. "Tallal, you don't have anything over on me any more... I am now going to be a father, too!"

They exchange a warm hug. "My friend and I have been praying for this for a long time now. God is great!" Tallal exclaims.

The two are exactly where they want to be in life, living side by side, providing for and raising their families next to each other. Work is going well, and the world seems to be slowly mending. New York continues to grow at a rapid rate, her streets filled with diversity, the skies seeming to lower as skyscrapers are built quickly. The Irish continue to immigrate *en masse*, bringing along a willpower, along with the Italians, to build cities and create new parishes of various ethnicities, all living life in unity.

When the next Christmas arrives, it becomes a celebration of many things. In Hober's house, Christmas trees are trimmed in shiny tinsel, the doorways adorned in Christmas lights. The biggest gift of the season: International trade from the United States increased throughout 1946, ensuring future work for construction workers as well as businessmen. Manhattan with its architectural pride, the Rockefeller Center, leaves room for other avenues for tall buildings. Life grows upward, as well. This creates the idea of building a World Trade Center. The news of this expansion sets the future in motion. Hober quits the shipyard to take a construction job on the new World Trade Center towers; there will eventually be two of them.

Because of climbing the Tatra Mountains and further up into the high Carpathians, Hober holds no fear of heights. While he is very anxious to begin work, the project of the World Trade Center keeps being put on hold, eventually not starting until the latter part of the 1960s – by which time Hober raises his boy and girl. Sylvia's wish has come true; Hober has his son and she her girl.

On New Year's Eve, the kitchen fills with more and more people as celebrations continue outside. Fireworks set sparkle to the New York City skyline as the young children sit wide-eyed in awe, Tallal and his family joining Hober. wreaths, with one red candle in each window. The two men share a cherished life, aging together, life unspooling the future and making it one of happiness and the dual traditions of Orthodoxy and Islam, which both families and the kids share. The neighborhood is fully bursting with Eastern Europeans, as well as Brits and Italians.

Hober remains many years at the shipyard before construction finally begins on the World Trade Center. The shipyard provides him a very good living, and he earns and saves toward his son's university education. Stephen has no idea that his father has his future all mapped out. Hober only wants for Stephen to have what he didn't, a fine education. He keeps his intentions to himself; if he told Sylvia, she would laugh at Hober trying to run his son's life before Stephen is even grown. Hober still has occasional nightmares of the war and life in Poland, and the poverty he came from. This is not what he wants for his son; he will make the university education happen when Stephen comes of age.

On a long, dull winter full of gray overcast skies, Tallal is busily raising his children and running the eatery. Magna decides to take on "child minding", and opens her house to the children of mothers now working in the city. She turns their home into a center for caring for these children. Her life feels full and fulfilled, and the extra income is a blessing for the family.

One day, Hober sits down with his daughter, Elena. "All good things come to those who wait," he says. She wants a new dress for the school dance. Sylvia has purchased material from the shops and will sew a beautiful dress without her knowing. Hober purchases a proper pair of shoes to match the dress… and once at the dance, Elena becomes the center of attention. She's also very proud of her parents and their dedication to her and her brother.

Chapter Fourteen

In 1966, ground is broken to build the World Trade Center. Hober attends the opening ceremony, which feels more like a day of great celebration. From two deep holes in the ground, a pair of giant towers will arise to bind America with Europe in international trade, a development that leaves New York, and Hober, brimming with pride. First, the United Nations. Now, the World Trade Center.

Hober and his family continue to grow in togetherness with Tallal's family in their settled lives. Relatives visit often from Sag Harbor. Stephen finishes up high school and begins university, where he will spend the next six years before graduating. He does well with his marks, yet Hober always thinks he can do better. One day, when Stephen is home for a short break, Hober rubs his chin with anticipation and asks, "How is your schooling? Do you think you will graduate with honors?"

"Dad? C'mon, can you give me a break?" Stephen asks. "I'm doing the best I can. Please don't break out the World War II stories again on how bad you had it, you and Tallal. Why don't you and Mom move from this house, for God's sake. It's worn out and old!"

"Son, we don't get rid of things because they become old. Your mom and I like this house, so kid, worry about yourself. And get good grades, okay?"

As he uses the word "kid," Hober thinks back to Mike, the pilot who flew he and Tallal to Amsterdam. That's what Mike called him, but after saying it to his own son, it takes Hober back to Poland and Amsterdam and all the things he's spent twenty years trying to forget. *Young peoples these days have no idea how hard life could be,* he thinks to himself.

Wars are ugly, leaving scars and wounds that often never heal. Yet those scars are exactly what can drive a person to succeed. Hober lives as honorably as he can, with God, his faith and nature aiding in the creation of such a man. He tries to pass this along to his children in a land of instant gratification. America is a well of everything a person could want, which still feels new to Hober – even after all this time. He wants what is best for his children, no matter what, even if it means reciting the liturgy on Sundays at Holy Trinity, or doing something charitable for others.

Sylvia loves Hober for all of this, and as they begin to grow into their later life, she understands much more how he came to be. She thinks of their years of marriage, all those winter nights listening to Hober's stories of he and Tallal, the deaths of Pia and his family, village life in Hoslava, and the people he helped along the way. These people did not cross his path by accident, she realizes; it was all God's will.

Hober will never forget Father Dominik, Angelica or Lars, his childhood friends, or the tundra and its animals, lakes and seasons. They formed Hober into exactly who he is. Stephen now resembles him in some ways. While pretending not to care about his father's past, he certainly has listened to his journey, and secretly hopes to be the man his father is – and to be recognized as that man by Hober.

Another year passes quickly. Sylvia's health begins to

decline; she suffers several heart attacks. Her stout French heritage helps her pull through, and the children grow much closer to her, Hober and family life. New York is full of temptations for young people, yet Hober's and Sylvia's endless dedication has resulted in two children who truly try to put family first. They love family life.

When Stephen arrives home from university after graduating, he and Hober spend time in the work shed, which has replaced the vegetable garden that fed them for many years. They create chairs, based on Polish woodworking styles, and donate them to new immigrants moving into the neighborhood. In doing this, Hober shows Stephen a charitable side. Elena goes to nursing school, her mother's poor health a huge motivator, and eventually becomes the head nurse of the cardiac unit at a nearby hospital.

Stephen also has fallen in love with a girl from Germany. Hober has a very hard time with the coupling... the word "German" singes his memory like a stray ember. He thinks of the Nazi ugliness, how they filled the camps with those they thought to be "less." While he struggles, he keeps his feelings secret, deep within him. His son's happiness matters most. He has already graduated with an international business degree and may one day travel to Europe. Perhaps he will even travel to Poland and visit Hoslava and the monuments of war, the concentration camps and museums that now hold the belongings of the persecuted. Perhaps one day, Hober thinks, Stephen will truly understand what his father went through.

Sophia's most recent heart attack has taken most of her strength. She becomes more reclusive, rarely going outdoors. Tallal cooks her foods with healing spices, but now she refuses to indulge him or his cooking. She spends most of her time in bed. Hober keeps working on the World Trade Center construction site to keep that paycheck ongoing.

Stephen marries Anna, and within a year, they welcome a baby boy. This is a joy to dear Hober. The heritage of family keeps growing, and traditions remain in place. Out at Sag Harbor, his cousins tend to their fields and homestead. The family even opens a small vineyard, producing late harvest wines. It is a good life for them. It seems America's basket of life keeps giving and giving.

The seasons switch to late autumn. The winds kick up a little more heavily as loose papers drift on the breeze along the streets of the city. Central Park is sprinkled in warm colors as vendors sell their harvest of sweet warm chestnuts. It seems a little more damp than usual as Hober works outdoors at the World Trade Center. The towers begin to take shape, high in the sky. Older, outdated buildings are removed from the site, which saddens him. Nothing old should be torn down.

Everything carries value these days. Hober's sense of life is more profound than it once was; the knowledge of that fine line is always there. Sylvia's health never leaves his thoughts.

Tallal's life is rich and full. Magna's "child minding" business has taken off in a big way; she now owns several of what she calls "daycare" services, and Tallal's eatery has become very popular with New Yorkers. His children grow up to become a doctor and photographer, both very successful. His life is far more than he ever could have imagined. Some relatives have even left Pakistan and now live in the neighborhood. Small white and yellow houses run along the oak-lined streets, speaking of the simplicity of a gentle day, still so very much noticed.

The two neighbors continue to tend to each other, even after all these years. If a tree falls, Hober aids Tallal in its removal. When the autumn leaves drop to their fullest, Tallal collects them for Hober. Brothers they will always be.

Their idyllic street ends at a cemetery holding men from all past wars. Hober walks to the end of the street to visit those fallen men, placing a stone by each marker he visits. Some are unmarked, a very sad thing for him. He recalls the elders of the village piled atop each other, like soiled rags, the Nazis ready to light them on fire and laugh while the bodies smoldered into ash. He still carries heavy memories, so the honor he holds for these soldiers that fought for their freedom – *my freedom,* he thinks – is beyond any words. He feels humbled by the white grave markers.

On the way back home, a stray beagle follows him from the cemetery. He is about a year old. The dog follows Hober to his front door. Hober tries to shoo him away, but the little dog won't have it. "Oh all right, then come in," he says with a soft sigh.

The little dog runs into the bedroom and quickly lays down with Sylvia, as if she were his long lost owner. It brings a wide smile to her face; Hober realizes this dog is what she needed. "I will name you Pierre," Sylvia says.

"Pierre? Ha ha ha ha Sylvia… he is not French, that is plain as day." Hober's voice twinges with sarcasm.

"Why not, Hober? I named him Pierre – and Pierre it is. After all, whose dog does he want to be? Yours or mine? He ran straight to me." Sylvia punctuates her words with a cough.

Hober smiles, thankful her spunk has returned.

Pierre becomes a part of the family. The year-old beige and white dog provides the lightness they need, and he goes everywhere with Hober and also on family functions. Little Pierre begins to frequent Sag Harbor and dives straightaway into the ocean, swimming as if he was born a salty dog.

Their small home again becomes a happy place. They have great neighbors in Tallal and Magna, the street is lively when it should be, but also quiets down at the right time. The neighborhood now houses several small ethnic shops, including an Italian place for mamma's take-away home cooking. There is also a British fish and chips shop, and a Middle Eastern grocery, with exotic foods as their specialty. This pleases Hober, makes him feel more international, which further broadens his mind.

Brooklyn grows quickly as well. Down at the World Trade Center, Hober and the others finish Tower One. Tower Two will soon be underway.

When summer ends, Stephen leaves for a five-week business trip to Europe. His first stop is Poland and his second, Germany, to visit Anna's family. Hober spends the entire time eagerly awaiting his son's return. He knows no harm will come to Stephen, yet his memories of Poland remain red with blood. The memories of the tundra and mountains fade as he ages, but he seems to more deeply recall the people who were killed. Hober finds himself falling into a delayed sort of depression, all the things that happened back then now affecting him in strange ways. Why is feeling the war more *now?* At home, Sylvia's health begins to decline again, and Tallal is so busy at the restaurant the two barely see each other, while Magna babysits her grandchildren uptown when not running her daycare centers. Hober's best friend now is Pierre, the beagle. With Elena's life hectic at the hospital, he truly misses evening meals with the family.

When there are hold-ups on the construction site, Hober travels to Sag Harbor, which he finds a refuge. Sylvia now rarely leaves the house, which results in Hober and Pierre traveling together often. The ocean air does something unique for him – it calms his mind. He works in the family vineyards, picking grapes, emptying his mind.

Finally, Stephen returns from Europe with some news: he is receiving a promotion and will be working in the World Trade Center! Hober's intuition begins to bother him, a feeling he hasn't had since the war. He feels lonely for the days of simplicity and laughter and time with absolutely nothing to do. His work at the construction site has lasted years, the towers now emerging as buildings of great importance. He knows they will stand out from the other buildings, and he and the other builders will always look upon them with great pride. When they are done, people of all ethnicities will work in the towers, united in their workplace.

Hober also appreciates the common bond that now exists between America and Europe – and that is to watch each succeed economically. Hober is proud of the work he and the others do. He's especially proud of those who climb the steel ribs of the buildings, the Steel Walkers, mostly crazy Irishmen who get a bird's eye view from the beams they weld together with heat and wild sparks.

Sylvia's final heart attack kills her. Hober buries her in the cemetery at the end of the street, he walks home alone, the oaks lining the small road, noticing how the facades of the small homes have changed over the past twenty-five years, some now painted bright purples and orange. Some of the oaks have even fallen, to be replaced by willows.

After Sylvia's funeral, Hober arrives home to find everyone together. Pierre wags his tail at the visitors, unaware that Sylvia is not coming home. The house is somber. Tallal keep to himself, not knowing what to say to his friend. Life is changing, and it saddens him.

Stephen enters the kitchen and pours himself a glass of water from the tap. "Dad, come live with us," he says.

Hober flashes a sad smile. "No son, I'm okay. I like our home and I have work to go to. I'm okay," he mutters as Elena makes coffee for the guests.

The feeling is all too familiar. When Angelica moved away all those years ago, he felt sorrowful. When Pia was murdered, he deeply grieved. Now Sylvia gone, and the sorrows feel much like the day the harvest fire killed his family. *God is good, God is good, Theotokos is in charge,* he thinks to himself.

Finally, the family leaves. When Pierre jumps into Stephen's car, Hober finds himself truly alone. The house is too quiet. He walks outside and looks up at the sky. "Hard to believe this is the same sky floating over Poland," he says.

The stars are brighter than usual, and the night sky very clear. By taking a step into the street and glancing to his left, he can also see the glow of Manhattan's skyline, the city lights. They ease his loneliness a bit. Later, Tallal brings over a sweet and Turkish coffee, reminding his friend, "I am still there for you and always will be, no matter how busy life gets."

The next day, Hober returns to work. He knows his mind needs to keep busy. The Twin Towers are taking their final form, and he finds solace in that achievement. Stephen is offered another promotion, which is also the offer to work in the Trade Center. Hober feels hesitation, even though he knows the Second Tower inside and out; he has spent the past several years working on it. Opening Day will soon arrive, and with it another celebration, this time an international celebration. Elena's work also keeps her very busy, worrying Hober about his other wish for her – to find a good man to marry and have children with.

Stephen has become a keen young man, happily married to Anna. The promotion comes at the right time. They need a larger home as their family is growing and the extra space is very much needed. Like his father, he is a good money saver. One day, he hopes to open his own firm and deal with China, something that would make Hober truly proud.

Hober thinks of his life. It has gone the way it was meant to go. His ambitions were to climb the Carpathians, map out a new passageway to the Ukraine, and walk the mountainside with Tallal – the exact thing that set his life in the other direction. Had he and Tallal kept going, they would have perished, for sure. His grand plan of life reflects his strong will and the power of hope, the driving force of his spirit, a spirit now passed along to his children.

Brooklyn has very little green space left, which leaves Hober to often daydream about Poland and the tundra, the lake and seasons, the hardships of the village, friends that led him exactly to where he is. Without their support, he may have remained in Hoslava and been imprisoned eventually in a camp, like the one he found in the forest. Karma surely works in mysterious ways.

After Sylvia's passing, Tallal spends most of the time at the restaurant and with his family, but often brings Hober leftovers from the evening menu. Hober is grateful for both his friend and work, though unsure of what he will do once the Twin Towers are completed. Maybe return to the shipyard? Or possibly go back to Poland and Hoslava, something he never thought he would entertain? Brooklyn and New York have been so good, yet as he tries to carry on without his wife, he misses the tundra. He has helped so many and kept so many safe that now he feels it might be time to return, the last action in his own healing process. Stephen and Elena can always come to visit, and Pierre has adopted Stephen since Sylvia's death, so he doesn't have to worry about the dog. Stephen and Anna love that Pierre was Sylvia's sweet beagle and companion during the last part of her illness. The dog reminds them of her tender heart.

On top of that, the neighborhood changes again. A few bungalows are torn down, and others are repainted in fashionable colors. Hober refuses to change his little home. The garden is plowed under and his work shed sits idle, the front yard now showing sparse bare areas, when once a perfect yard was his pride and joy. Thank God, he thinks, that he still has work, though construction of the Towers is nearly over. A few more weeks, and the grand opening will be headline news in *The New York Times*. Hober all but bursts with pride; he knows his welded beams and connecting stairwells to the walls are a big part of the building. He put his heart into each weld. He also etched his name in a secret spot on the eleventh floor, dedicating it to Poland and her people.

On April 4, 1973, the World Trade Center officially opens. They are the tallest buildings in the world, and what pride New York has! The doors and glass windows gleam brightly, even on cloudy days. The elevators go up and down endlessly, the buildings seemingly content to house offices of corporations and businesses in both International and New York City style. There are hot dog stands and sit-down restaurants. On a typical day, fifty thousand people will work there. It amazes Hober as he marvels at the magnitude of this achievement, though he never gives himself credit with the other contractors who built the structures.

Stephen is given an office on the thirtieth floor of Tower One. Hober tries his best not to picture his son working so high above the ground. He carries a secret uneasiness. The Towers are spectacular, something he never thought possible. He had been to a city before, Warsaw, but it was rubble by the time he arrived, the once Bohemian city brought to its knees by Hitler's bombs and shells. It gives Hober a stark reminder that whenever so many people can come together in one place, it can create unease and danger. Night after night, the war and Poland come back to him in nightmares. Sylvia was his mental anchor, but now, he spins in his dreams of times past... perhaps it is a sign.

While Hober adjusts to world changes, he remains in the same house. However, Tallal and family move to the suburbs and enjoy that life, commuting daily to the city, often inviting Hober to stay with them and enjoy the greenery. He visits Tallal and family, never wanting to stay too long. He never wants to be too far from Sylvia and visits her grave daily before or after work. He returns to the shipyard for part-time work. Elena visits weekly while Stephen dives into his job full force. He and Anna now have two children, who are the light of Hober's eyes. He is a "Dziadek" –a grandfather – and there is not much else so honorable. His life begins to revolve around his grandchildren, which gives him more time with Stephen and also Pierre.

Dinner remains a special time. He sits at the end of his table, counting the heads of his family, breaking open an egg and thinking about the lovely simplicities of life, a warm fire, good family and food. Those are the only things he ever truly needed, and he had them. He misses Sylvia and always will. Angelica was his childhood love, then Pia his first true love; her murder devastated him. Never did he think he would find love again, let alone in America.

"Stephen, my son, I am so very proud of you," Hober says, pulling him in and giving him a strong one-armed hug. "My boy is a success."

Hober's voice quivers a bit. He holds back tears; the pride he holds for his son is profound. Life in the village was laborious during the winter months, rationing the harvest, storing foods for the prolonged darkness. Early on, this taught Hober about the humility life demands – what he truly wanted to pass along to Stephen and Elena. He feels successful in doing that; now he can grow old and witness his family's growth and successes.

Stephen is eager to arrive at work. Once he sits in his office, he looks out. The New York skyline seems to have always included the World Trade Center as part of it. He enjoys the fact that he is a big part of the beginning of such a fantastic endeavor. The hum of the office feels a part of the heartbeat of the business world, the international business world. To him, there is no larger reward for his diploma and his years at the university. He is a very proud man with a heart as large as his father's. He and Antonie, one of the Tower Two maintenance men, have become great friends; Hober's lifelong devotion to Tallal is also instilled in Stephen. It's the knowing of true friends, the gifts of friendship being the very thing that can, later in life, provide the strength we all need now and then. *The support of friendship provides the crutch,* Stephen thinks, *when we all sometimes are limping from dealing with the human condition. To share life and foods and even death are the ties that bind us to each other.*

More years pass, right into the 21st century and the year 2001. Life drifts by on an even keel. The grandchildren grow, and Hober's days now fill with taking them to school. The school is located near their neighborhood, with Hober's house several blocks away. He insists on driving them, even on warm sunny days. Hober will risk nothing. With him aging, if something else happened to the family... any more loss would kill him.

Stephen pokes at Hober's overprotectiveness now and then. "Dad, the kids are fine," he says. "Let them be kids and allow them to walk to school."

He sounds like a broken record to Hober, who ignores him. At seven thirty every morning, he picks up and drops off the kids at the school door. When school ends, he returns to collect the children and again safely stuff them in the back seat of his Pontiac. The black leather seat shifts a little to their tiny frames while Hober drives them home, a grand smile on his face. But first, they stop at his house – and go inside for a few minutes, where he shares a secret he keeps between he and the kids. They stand at the base of the icon of

Mother Mary and pray for the family. Afterwards, they all receive a sweet, either apple dumplings with warm cream or a sticky pudding, normally tapioca. Now and then, Hober makes them chocolate pudding against Stephen's will. Hober is the epitome of a Polish *Dziadek*.

During the wee hours of September 11, Hober awakens at three a.m., screaming. He has a nightmare involving Stephen. Though fragmented, his dream was brightly illuminated in white light, explosive, with shouting and screaming, loud noises and explosions. He doesn't fall back asleep, and as the sun rises, he cannot shake the feeling. *Something terrible is going to happen...*

He phones Stephen at seven a.m. No answer. He figures Stephen is in the middle of his commute to the Twin Towers. Perhaps he had to go to work early and simply cannot answer the phone. The fact Stephen's office is in Tower Two still marvels Hober. But the clock ticks loudly and the sound begins to trouble Hober even more, the exaggerated loudness, nearly simulating time's reminder that Stephen has not phoned him back. He waits and waits... waiting... waiting ... his mind troubled with memories and the nightmare.

Hober then phones Tallal, whose new restaurant is near the Towers. He does not answer, either.

The house seems too quiet. Since Sylvia died, Hober has kept the radio on constantly. When Tallal moved to the suburbs, and Stephen and Elena moved away nearby, yet not close enough for Hober's likings, he needed the companionship of the radio. Once again, he drops off the children at school, adjusts the radio dial in his car – and hears an announcer break in, his tone of voice upsetting. Hober turns the volume up. The announcer continues:

"Two jets have been hijacked! We are not sure yet what is taking place... further information will be available shortly."

This isn't real, this can't be real! Hober thinks. His mind flips through memories like book pages, returning to Poland and the war and broadcasts of London's bombing and Warsaw's destruction, Italy's devastation, the occupations of Greece and France... so many gone for such a terrible reason. Now it seems that old war has followed him; the world has begun to roil in chaos again, with the Middle East on everyone's mind.

Today, life is about to change for humanity once again, with hard working people being victimized once more.

Hober pulls the car to the side of the road. The announcer returns to the airwaves: "Another plane is off-course, apparently headed to Cleveland, Ohio. The Air Force has been called, yet there are no details as of yet..."

Hober's heart begins to pound in his chest. "Oh my God, what is going on?" he shouts to himself in the car.

"...Another plane is off course, heading towards Washington D.C..." The announcer's voice is shaken. Just as he finishes, his voice switches to a combination of shock and severe sadness: "There are reports from people on the streets of New York. A plane has just struck the Twin Towers. We are not sure yet of the details, whether this was intentional or an accident. A plane has struck Tower One. People are running away from the towers, and emergency squads are responding. They are blanketed in hot, heavy smoke."

Hober breath staggers as he remains in the car. He rolls the windows down, in case he can hear any sounds coming from the city. His mind races. Should he cross the Brooklyn

Bridge and drive into the city? See for himself what is happening? *It's impossible – the Towers cannot be a target!*

Then it hits him: Stephen never returned his call. He grips the steering wheel tightly as the announcer returns with even worse news:

"Oh my God! Another plane has just struck Tower Two! It seems the planes have exploded on contact – inside the Towers!"

Hober rolls up his car window. He screams in sorrow, his cries becoming wails. His son, his sweet, sweet son… how will he know if he is okay? How will he know if he survived?

The tragedy pulls New York down to its knees. Her sister Towers are under attack. The skyline fills with heavy smoke that lofts over and across the city. The towers remain standing, as if trying to give everyone the chance and time to get out.

At 9.59 a.m., three hours after Hober first tried to call Stephen, Tower One collapses. The South Tower. Less than an hour has passed since the plane struck it. At 10.28 a.m., the North Tower collapses as well. A total of two thousand seven hundred and sixty-three people lose their lives.

Stephen is one of them.

As Hober later learned, after evacuating the South Tower, Stephen re-entered to aid those who couldn't make it down the stairwells on their own, his friend, Antonie, one of those people. These were the very stairs Hober helped to create with his welding skills, where he secretly welded his name under the steps. Stephen fell inside the tower as it collapsed on those still trying to escape.

The buildings are reduced to hot melting iron, glazed by

dark smoke and human hope and will. The terrorists have taken so much. As in any terror attack, the format for September 11 was to "take and terrorize", and the devious people did just that, a stark reminder of war – and of men who, emptied of all human emotions, can take life accompanied by their own deaths.

In the car, Hober realizes what he has just heard. "Not Stephen, he can't be gone!" A few days later, the memorial for Stephen is held at Saint Nicholas. There are no bodily remains, only ash lying in more ash, among those lost in the South Tower. New York is in anguish, the world in empathy for those under attack and killed. And now, Hober is forced to bury an empty casket. He wants Stephen to have an Orthodox service, which he needs as well. Elena and Anna, Stephen's wife, are buried inside their own grief.

The family will never be the same again.

A few months pass. Winter arrives. The family has learned not to bother Hober when he is in a solitary state of mind.
He collects the mail from the postbox. Inside is an envelope containing Oplatki for the holiday meal. The meal Stephen would have been a part of. He breaks the Oplatki on Christmas Eve, the white wafer baked unleavened by the Sisters of Trinity convent. Hober follows this Christian tradition as his own father once did. But this year, there is no son to whom to pass the wafer. He does not set the table in Polish blues. The eggs remain unboiled and the bread unbaked.

Hober feels he has lost more than half of himself, which died with Stephen. His home would not be transferred to his son in inheritance any more. Elena is not interested in an inheritance; she is content living in her own home. This leaves Hober feeling even more distraught.

One day, he's had enough. He places the house on the market. The real estate agent hands him a list of requirements, financial requirements to retain her. Hober signs the papers, handing her the payment. Within a month, the house is sold. Hober donates most of his belongings and rents a small apartment inside the city, leaving Sylvia in the cemetery in Brooklyn.

Spring comes once more. The scented cherry blossom air slips Hober back to Poland. He again sees the table set for Easter by his mother and sister, and his father's hard-working hands. He sees the calluses of that hard work, the forest and the lake. He longs for Poland again. He longs for the tundra. It is time to return home.

"Dad, you can't go back to Poland!" Elena shouts when Hober tells her.

"Yes, I can – and I am," he replies sharply. He has endured enough pain to last several lifetimes. He feels he truly belongs back home.

"Elena, I love you, my daughter, I love the grandchildren, and I love Stephen. I think now it is time to go home," he says again, more softly this time, the words spreading into the spring air.

"Well, okay then, Dad. I guess I can't stop you. I love you, too, Dad."

Elena feels a big sense of loss once more: her mother is gone, now Stephen is gone, and the family is not the same.

Soon, Hober purchases a ticket for Amsterdam. From there, he will travel by train to Warsaw and then back to Hoslava. Over the years, he'd read about Poland and its rebuilding, the restructuring after the war. It once again populated enough to gain the title of "town"; this is where he returns. Poland will always be home, he realizes, no matter the dreams and hopes of a young man who lost so much.

He says goodbye to Tallal and his family. "We will always be brothers," he reminds Tallal.

Chapter Fifteen

Hober lands in Amsterdam, boards his train to Warsaw and then the connecting train to Hoslava. The city lights fade into the tundra. When he sees Hoslava, he realizes it is not just a town, but a small city; she reached so many that she is now a city in every aspect. His heart fills with memories of family and the happiness each season brought, no matter how hard the times. He thinks of Father Dominik, his friends, the people he helped escape from the Nazis, the mountains and their echoing from the avalanches. He never realized how much he left behind, concentrating more on losses and not gains. But the tundra gave and still gives so much to the very air they all breathe, and the energy of nature, the snow and animals.

The streets of Hoslava are joyous. There are many cafes and shops, and the church is still standing in the very place it was when he left for Poland. The church bells chime as people gather for vespers, and he notices a new church in the city square, a Catholic church named Saint Barbara's. This pleases him, for religion doesn't have any walls, yet God has many houses.

The night feels like Christmas, though it is not. Autumn has fallen away with the leaves of the old oaks. Homes and shops are warmed by inviting hearths. Hober recognizes a man sitting at a small table in the café. The man looks over at

Hober, and then his face fills with surprise.

"Lars?" Hober asks.

"You old dog, Hober! I can't believe it's you," Lars shouts. "Come in, have a seat… would you like some warm tea?"

Lars looks so much older, yet his voice sounds like the thirteen-year-old Hober knew. He loves the idea that Lars, too, returned to Hoslava. "Lars! Your eyes look the same, but I can't say the rest of you looks the same as when I last saw you."

With that, Hober slips back into his old joking self. Once again, Lars pulls the better side out of Hober, his sense of humor returning quickly. Hober is more than happy to see his old friend.

"Man, where have you been, Hober? I have been looking for you for a few years now.

"Where did you end up?" Lars speaks a mile a minute.

"Slow down, Lars. I was living in America. I have two children… well, did have two children. Stephen died in the attack on the World Trade Center in New York." He begins to tear up.

"Man, Hober, I am very sorry to hear that."

Lars speaks the same emphatic statement many have used since Stephen's death, but really, what can anyone say? Death is death and it brings inside a lifetime of grief.

"I'm okay, Lars. It's good to be back. I was thinking of a good hike tomorrow. Would you like to join me? I'm thinking of that old concentration camp. You want to tag along?"

"Hober, they tore that down long ago."

"Oh, I suppose it was for the better," Hober replies.

"Now what about that hike tomorrow?"

"We are not young men any longer," Lars says. "Do you think it is wise to hike into the forest?"

"Lars, I am an old man, and I have returned home. In that, I feel a sense of youth again. I would like to walk into the forest, listening to the distant sounds of the avalanches, and perhaps return to the site of the camp where Pia died." His voice weakens as he finishes.

"Okay, I will go with you, then afterward, let's just sit and reminisce about the good days, when we were all together in our misfit pack of friends." Lars seems upset about something, maybe the sobering thought about mortality and how time speeds up as we get closer to the end.

The next morning, Lars and Hober set out with knapsacks filled with eggs, cheese and bread, a warm pair of socks in case they muddy the ones they are wearing, plus a lamp and rain jackets, which they never packed in the old days. At their ages, they realize all of the "what if's" that can take place. Youth carries the unprepared and eager, but age creates wisdom.

The day is bright, a gentle sun suspended above them. The forest seems to have changed – or is it that Hober has changed? He can't decide. His youth is far off in the distance; the forest isn't nearly as dense as he recalled. The lake is smaller than he remembered, and the slabs of concrete that once made the walls of the concentration camp are much smaller as well. This confuses Hober; where has his memory gone? The place of Pia's death, behind the fourth building, is no longer there. The camp seems an entirely different place now.

They hike for several hours, tiring both of them. The

canopy is shallow as the sun bleeds through the branches. They take time to eat their lunches as they sit on huge boulders. They enjoy eggs, bread, and short glasses of vodka. Hober sits quietly. So does Lars. They take in the forest, the sky, the memories.

As it turns out, Lars never married; his profession became his life. He fell in love once, though, and the pain of loss proved too much to give into, so he chose a good profession and a life of travel, only to return to Hoslava. Lars is content, though. Through him, Hober learns that Father Dominik passed away after a lifetime of aiding others and being one of the best priests the bishop had the pleasure of working with. After retiring, he passes soon thereafter in a lovely home for retired priests. Angelica also passed, about a year before Hober returned; her life was not always easy, but very fulfilled.

Perhaps Hoslava has changed most of all. The streets are now paved, and street lamps hang above the passing cars. Yet, as the modern world continues to grow into the town, Hoslava holds onto its charm. It is old world, yet modern enough to draw in new citizens. Hober is proud of his city, part of the rich cultural life of Poland, which still teeters now and then on the "what ifs", never cemented in the securities other countries hold.

The passageway to the Ukraine, once considered nearly impossible, is now a thriving motorway with service and observation areas for viewing the valleys and tundra. The tunnel is lined with dim safety lights, and the slot car rhythm of motor pedestrians clearing the tunnels and entering the Ukraine.

Hober's dream to become a world-class mountaineer

faded into the realities of the war, the survival of Poland and Europe, and the challenges of rebuilding and restructuring political systems. Such tasks went on and still go on, very unappreciated. The movement of cultural traditions reignites in importance to Polish families; whether at home or abroad, they warm Hober's heart. He thinks of the Orthodox church's belief: "All things have soul."

Life is built on family and children and the church. No one is condemned by a fierce God, yet they are loved by a forgiving one. Man creates war, not God; war develops from man's choices, from free will. War is ugly.

His faith in the higher power of God has been obvious his entire life. He never blames God for natural disasters or war, even the World Trade Center disaster that killed so many innocent people, nor the death of his family in the festival fire, or his son and wife. Hober never blamed God for any of this. He knows life unravels within the human condition.

He is happy to see Lars again. They enjoy a day of chatting about the past and walking the streets of Hoslava.

That night, he watches an elder descend from the mountains. The man proudly rides in his horse-drawn cart, decorated in bright red and blue streamers. Modern life has yet to find the elder. Hober smiles and nods. This elder's life is how they all once lived.

Hober falls ill the day after visiting Lars. Children of the women Hober once knew catch wind that he is not well; some are relatives of the young kids he liberated on the road from Warsaw. They tend to him in shifts. Elena is notified and flies to Hoslava, her first trip to Poland, and sits at her father's side as he draws his last breath.

Hober is buried in the cemetery outside Hoslava. Elena

instructs that he be buried in the section of the graveyard where Hitler's victims lie in rest. His marker is neither grand nor posh. It is a simple granite stone from the Tatra Mountains. Here Hober rests eternally, under the watchful eye of the tundra.